Henry Harland

Mademoiselle Miss

And other Stories

Henry Harland

Mademoiselle Miss
And other Stories

ISBN/EAN: 9783744750509

Printed in Europe, USA, Canada, Australia, Japan

Cover: Foto ©Andreas Hilbeck / pixelio.de

More available books at **www.hansebooks.com**

MADEMOISELLE MISS

AND OTHER STORIES

BY

HENRY HARLAND

LONDON   WILLIAM HEINEMANN

MDCCCXCIII   BEDFORD STREET W.C.

CONTENTS

MADEMOISELLE MISS

MADEMOISELLE MISS.

" Mais que diable allait-elle faire en cette galère ? "

PARIS is the gloomiest town in Christendom to-day,—though it is a lovely day in April, and the breeze is full of softness, and the streets are gay with people,—and the Latin Quarter is quite the dullest bit of Paris : Mademoiselle Miss left last night for England.

We all know what it is like when a person who has been an absorbing interest in our lives suddenly goes away : how, apart from the immediate pang of the separation and the after-pain of more or less consciously missing the fugitive, there is a wide, complex, dim underworld of emotion, that may be compared to the thorough-bass of a sad

tune, and seems in some sort to relate itself
to the whole exterior universe. The sun
rises as usual, but the sunlight is not the
same. Other folk, apparently unconcerned,
pursue the accustomed tenor of their way;
but we are vaguely surprised that this should
be the case,—surprised, and grieved, and a
little resentful. We can't realise without an
effort how completely exempt they are from
the loss that has befallen us ; and we feel
obscurely that their air of indifference is
either sheer braggadocio, or a symptom of
moral insensibility. The truth of the matter
is, of course, that our departing friend has
taken with him not his particular body and
baggage only, but an element from the earth
and the sky, and a fibre from ourselves.
Everything is subtly, incommunicably altered. We wake up to a changed horizon :
and our distress is none the less keen because the changeling bears a formal resem-
blance to the vanished original.

So ! Mademoiselle Miss has gone to Eng-

land ; and to-day it is a new and an unfamil-
iar and a most dismal Paris that confronts
the little band of worshippers she has left
behind her.   Indeed, it was already a new
Paris that the half dozen of us who had
assembled at St. Lazare to see her off,
emerged into from the station last night,
after her train had rolled away.   We found
a corner seat for her in a third-class compartment reserved for *dames seules ;* and
while some of us attended to the register-
ing of her box, others packed her light
luggage into the rack above her head; and
this man had brought a bunch of violets,
and that a book for her to read ; and Jean con-
tributed a bottle of claret, and Jacques a nap-
kin full of sandwiches : and taken for all in
all, we were the forlornest little party you
can easily conceive of, despite our spasmodic
attempts at merriment.   We grouped ourselves round the window of her carriage,—
stopping the way thereby, though not with
malice aforethought, for such other solitary

ladies as might wish to enter,—whilst Miss
smiled down upon us from eyes that were
perilously bright ; and we sought to defy the
ache that was in our hearts, by firing off brisk
little questions and injunctions, or abortive
little jests.

"Sure you've got your ticket all right ? "

" You must make a rush for a berth directly you reach Dieppe."

" Mind you write the moment you arrive. "

"Oh, we'll get news of her through Don
Antonio."—This was meant as facetious,
and we all laughed, though rather feebly :
Don Antonio being an aged Italian model
whom Miss had painted a good deal, and
between whom and herself there was
humorously supposed to have taken place
a desperate flirtation.

We were constantly lapsing into silence,
however ; and for the last five minutes we
scarcely spoke at all. We simply waited
there, moving uneasily among ourselves,
and gazed up at her. She kept on smiling

at us; but it was a rueful smile, and we could easily see that the tears weren't far behind it. Then suddenly a bell rang; the officials shouted "*En voiture;*" there was a volley of good-byes, a confusion of hand-shaking; the engine shrieked; her arm was drawn in through the window; the train moved; and Miss was gone.

We lingered for a moment on the platform, looking stupidly after the red lamp at the end of the last carriage, as it waned swiftly smaller and fainter in the distance.

Presently someone pulled himself together sufficiently to say, "Well, come on."

And we made our way out of the station into a Paris that was blank and strange. Aubémont (Adolphe) was frankly holding his pocket-handkerchief to his eyes; but we Anglo-Saxons chid and chaffed him till he put it out of sight.

"By Christopher! when I think of the way we treated that girl in the beginning!" cried Chalks, an American, whose lay-name is

Charles K. Smith, but he's called Chalks by
all his English-speaking fellow-craftsmen.

Whereat—"Oh, shut up!" came in chorus from the rest of us. We didn't care to
be reminded of those old days.

Then little Schaas-Keym, the Dutchman,
proposed that we should finish the evening,
and court oblivion, at the Galurin Cassé :
and we adopted his suggestion, and drank
beer, and smoked, and chattered, and ate
cold beef and pickles, till the place was closed,
at 2 A. M., when we returned to the Quarter,
six in a single cab.

Thus we managed to wear out last night
with sufficient comfort. We gave ourselves
no time, no chance, to think. We stood
together, and drowned our sorrow in the
noise we made. And then, by the time we
parted, we were sleepy, so that we could go
straight to our beds and forget everything.

But—this morning !

It is proverbially on the next morning
that a man's wound begins to hurt. For the

others, since I've seen none of them, I can
speak only by inference : in the morning our
little *cénacle* scatters to the four corners of the
town, not to be reunited till the hour of dinner ; but what reason is there to doubt that
the day will have treated them very much
as it has treated me ? And oh, the weary,
dreary, bright spring day it is ! The Luxembourg is fragrant with budding trees, and
vocal with half a thousand romping children ;
the Boule-Miche is at its liveliest, with a
ceaseless ebb and flow of laughing young
men and women ; the *terrasse* of the Vachette
is a mass of gleaming top-hats and flaunting
feminine bonnets ; and the sky overhead is
one smooth blue vault, and the sun is everywhere, a fume of gold : but the sparkle and
the joyousness of it all are gone. Turn
where I will, I find the same awful sense of
emptiness. The streets are deserted, in spite
of the crowds : I can hear my solitary footsteps echo gruesomely through them. Paris
is like Pompeii.

After luncheon, thinking to obtain relief by fleeing the Quarter (where every blessed stick and stone has its bitter-sweet association with her), I crossed the river, mixed with the throng in the Boulevard, sat for a while at the Café de la Paix.   But things were no whit better.   The sun shone with the same cheerless brilliancy ; the air touched one with the same light, uncomforting caress ; the laughter of the wayfarers had the same hollow ring.   A blight had fallen upon man and nature.   I came back to the Rue Racine, and its ghosts of her.

That exclamation of Smith's last night, to which we all cried taboo, really hit one of the salient points of the position : when I think of the way we treated her in the beginning ! Extenuating circumstances might be pleaded for us, no doubt.   It was only natural that we should have treated her so, if tradition and convention can make a thing natural—if it is natural that men should glare at a woman in a smoking-car-

riage, for example. And besides, she has
had her revenge. For that matter, she was
never conscious of our offences ; but she
has had her revenge, if to see us one by
one prostrate ourselves at her feet, humble
adorers, eager servitors,—if that may con-
stitute revenge. And then, we are told,
though our sins be as red as scarlet, if we do
truly repent, they shall be washed as white
as snow : and we have repented, goodness
knows how truly. All the same, forgiveness
without forgetfulness being but the guinea-
stamp without the gold, I wish I could forget the way we treated her in the beginning.

One is judged by the company one keeps ;
and she kept—ours. It is now some nine
months ago that she appeared in it, at the
Hôtel de l'Océan et de Shakespere, in the Rue
Racine. We were just hasty enough, un-
observant enough, blunt enough of perception, to judge her accordingly,—to take for
granted, in a casual, matter-of-course fash-

ion, that she would be a vessel of like clay to our own.

The entrance to the Hôtel de l'Océan et de Shakespere, a narrow, dark, ambiguous-looking entrance, is flanked by two tin signs. That at the right hand reads, " *Chambres et Cabinets Meublés ;*" that at the left, "*Pension de Famille.*" Call it a *Pension de Famille*, if you will : at the epoch when Mademoiselle Miss arrived among us, we were, to put it squarely, the most disreputable family in Europe.

Our proprietress, Madame Bourdon, was a gelatinous old person from Toulouse, with a pair of hazy blue eyes, a mottled complexion, a worldly-wise smile, an indulgent heart, and an extremely nasal accent. I speak of her as old; but she wasn't old enough to know better, apparently. At any rate she had a certain unbeneficed *abbé* perpetually hanging to her apron-strings, and she kept him to dinner half a dozen evenings in the week. Of her boarders all the

men were students, all the women *étudiantes*,
—which, being interpreted, I suppose means
students too. There were Mesdames Germaine, Fifine, Olga, Yvonne, Zélie, and
Lucile, —

"Whose names are six sweet symphonies,"—

and perhaps it was because Lucile was
her niece that Madame had dubbed her shop
a *pension de famille.* You paid so much for
your room and service, and then you could
take table d'hôte or not, as you elected. Most
of us took it, because it was only fifty francs
a month, *vin compris.* Our ladies dined
abroad a good deal, being inconstant quantities, according to the custom of their sex ;
but the men were almost always present in
full number. We counted seven : Chalks,
Schaas-Keym, Aubêmont, Jeanselme, Campbell, Norton, and myself. We formed a sort
of close corporation, based upon a com-
munity of tastes, interests, and circumstances. We were all "arts,"—except
Jeanselme, who was a "mines," with a

disordered tendency to break out in verse : we were all ridiculously poor, and we were all fond of bohemianising up and down the face of Paris.

One evening in September of last year, on entering our *salle-à-manger*, we beheld a stranger, an addition to our ranks ; and Madame, with a comprehensive gesture, introduced her to us in these terms : "*Une nouvelle, une anglaise, Mees, . . .*" Then she made awful hash of rather a long-winded English name : and we were content to accept the newcomer simply as Miss. The concierge and the servants, though, (to anticipate a little), treated Miss as a *petit-nom*, like Jane or Susan, and prefixed the title Mademoiselle. The pleonasm seemed a happy one, and we took it up : Mademoiselle Miss. On her visiting-card the legend ran, "Miss Edith Thorowether." It was probably as well, on the whole, that French lips should not too frequently have tackled that.

Now if she had been plain or elderly or
constrained in her bearing or ill-natured-
looking, no doubt we should have felt at
once the difference between her and ourselves, and understood her presence with us
as merely the outward and visible sign of
some inward and spiritual blunder. But, as
it happened, she was young and distinctly
pretty ; and she appeared to be entirely at
her ease ; and she smiled graciously in ac-
knowledgment of the somewhat cursory
nods with which we favoured her. We
hadn't the wit or the intuitions to recognise
her ease for the ease of innocence ; and our
hotel was *such* a risky box ; and ladies of
English or American origin were no especial
novelty in the Quarter ; and we didn't stop
to examine this one critically, or to consider ; and so things fell out in a way we
now find disagreeable to remember. It was
Saul who had strayed by hazard into the
midst of our prophetic councils ; and we
mistook him for one of our own prophetic

caste, and proceeded to demean and express ourselves in our usual prophetic manner. Fortunately, Saul's knowledge of our prophetic tongue was limited. We spoke the slang of the Boulevards; whilst the little French that Mademoiselle Miss was mistress of she had learned from Ollendorf and Corinne.

The situation was partially cleared up, I forget how long afterwards, by our discovering in her room, whither she had bidden us for an evening's entertainment, an ancient copy of a certain Handbook to Paris,— "the badge of all our tribe," as the tourist called it. On opening to its list of hotels (which somebody did by chance), we found the following note, with a pencil-mark against it : "Hôtel de l'Océan et de Shakespere, Rue Racine, chiefly frequented by visitors pursuing art-studies : well spoken-of and inexpensive." That explained it. Mademoiselle Miss had trusted to a guide that was ten years behind the times : so the date

on the title-page attested. And in ten years
how had the Hôtel de l'Océan et de Shakespere fallen from its respectable estate!—
unless, ten years ago, the editor of that
|most exemplary handbook had been egre-
|giously imposed upon. In his current edi-
tion the paragraph that I have cited does
not appear.

But to return to the evening of her arrival.
In our *salle-à-manger* there was a rigid divi-
sion of the sexes. The men sat on one side
of the long table, the women on the other,
with Madame and her *abbé* cheek by jowl at
the head. It was the only arrangement
Madame had been able to effect, whereby
to maintain amongst us something resem-
bling order. Mademoiselle Miss had a seat
assigned to her between Zélie and Yvonne,
nearly opposite Chalks and myself; and she
entered without embarrassment into conversation with all four of us. That is to say,
she responded as well as she could in her
broken classic French, and with perfect ami-

ability, to such remarks as we directed at her. Save in addressing Madame or the *abbé*, nobody ever thought of saying *vous* at our unceremonious board ; and Miss showed neither displeasure nor surprise when we included her in the prevailing *tu*. She had a quiet, sweet, English voice ; an extremely delicate complexion, pale rose merging into lily-white (which we, I dare say, assumed was due to a scientific management of rouge and powder) ; a pair of large gray eyes ; a lot of waving warm-brown hair ; and a face so smooth of contour, so soft and fine in texture, that one might have thought her a mere girl of eighteen,—or twenty at the utmost,—whereas, in point of fact, as we learned later on, she was twenty-three.

On this first evening of her arrival, however, neophyte though she was, we observed her with no special care, paid her no special attention, nor felt any special curiosity regarding her. Ladies of the quality we tacitly ascribed to her were such an old,

old story for us ; familiarity had bred
apathy ; we took her for granted very much
as we might have taken for granted an addition to the number of chairs in the room.
Besides, an attitude of *nil-admirari* towards
all things, and particularly towards all things
new, is the fashion of the Quarter ; an attitude of torpid omniscience, of world-weary
sophistication. We have seen everything,
dissected everything, satisfied ourselves that
everthing is stuffed with sawdust. We are *fin-
de-siècle*, we are *décadents*, and we are An-
glomaniacs to a man. To evince surprise at
anything, therefore, or more than a supremely
languid interest in anything, is what, when
we are on our guard, most of us would die
rather than do. Hence the questions that we
put to Miss were few, desultory, superficial,
and served in no wise to correct our mis-
appreciation of her ; whilst, together with the
affirmative propositions that we laid down,
they pre-supposed a point of view and a
past experience similar to our own.

Zélie, for example, asked her roundly (as
one of a trade to another) : " *Tu cherches
un collage, hein ?   On fais l'indépendante ?*"

Miss looked a little puzzled, but answered
tentatively, "*Non, pas collège.   Je suis ar-
tiste.*"

Whereat one or two of us stared, thinking
it meaningless ; one or two smiled, thinking
it doubly-meaning ; but the majority heeded
it not ; and no one paused to consider the
depths of ignorance (unless, indeed, ignorance of the French language) that the
reply might indicate.   I should perhaps add
that with us the young ladies who dance at
Bullier's, sing at the *concerts apéritifs*, or serve
in the *brasseries-à-femmes*, style themselves
artistes.

At the end of the dinner, when the stuff
that Madame Bourdon euphemistically calls
coffee was brought in, we all broke out in
loud accord with a song that time-honoured
custom has prescribed for the event and
moment.   We are never treated to this

beverage at the Hôtel de l'Océan et de Shakespere, except on the advent of a *nouveau* or a *nouvelle*, when it is charged to his or her account ; and here is the salute with which we hail it :—

A la recherch' de la paternité !
Chaforé ?
Accident arrivé
A l'amèr' Chicorée
Par liaison passagère
'Vec le père
Café.
Papa Café ?
Pas, pas café !

L'amèr' Chicorée est française,
Fill' de fermier,
Et pourtant,—comment donc,—ell' baise
Cet étranger,
Ce gros gaillard de païen
Pacha Café ?
Shocking—hein ?

Et le bébé,
Chaforé ?
C'reti'n,—
Baptisé
A main pleine
D'eau de Seine.

This atrocious doggerel, with its false
rhymes and impossible quantities, its bad
puns and equivocal suggestions, we sang
straight through, at the tops of our voices ;
and Mademoiselle Miss listened smiling.
How were we to know that she hadn't the
faintest inkling of what it was all about, and
that her smile betokened nothing deeper
than pleasure in our high spirits and amusement at our vociferous energy? By and by
she rose from the table, wished us a polite
good-evening, and left the room.

I think it was on the next night that we
made up a party to go to Bruant's, in the
Boulevard Rochechouart ; and Zélie, moved
by an impulse of kindness, turned to Miss,
and proposed that she should join us. Miss
asked what Bruant's was ; and Zélie answered vaguely, "*Comment, tu ne sais pas ?
Tant mieux, alors. Tu vas voir.*" And Miss
retired to put on her bonnet.

Thank goodness, if her acquaintance with
French was slight, her acquaintance with

the jargon talked and chanted at the Cabaret
du Mirliton was null. Otherwise, she must
always have remembered her visit there with
pain and humiliation, and she could never
have forgiven us for allowing her to make
one of our expedition. As a matter of fact,
however, she is able to recall the occasion
as that of a singularly jolly little adventure,
and is entirely unaware of the blame that
we deserved.

At the outcry of

" O-là-là,
C'tte gueule qu'elle a ! "

wherewith ladies crossing the threshold of
Bruant's establishment are welcomed, Miss
only smiled in a dazed way, never dreaming, I suppose, that it was meant for her and
her companions, but fancying that we had
entered in the middle of a noisy chorus.
Then, when we had secured places, and
ordered our bocks, I dare say she employed
a few minutes in glancing round her, and

receiving a general impression of the queer little room,—with its dark colouring, its profuse jumble of ornaments and paintings, its precious old Fifteenth Century fireplace, its giant *mirliton* suspended from the ceiling, its dubious clients, and its improbable orderer and master, handsome, brigandish-looking Aristide, in his scarlet neck-cloth, his patent-leather riding-boots and corduroy knicker-bockers : all visible through an atmosphere rendered opalescent by candlelight struggling with cigarette-smoke.

At Bruant's, as everybody knows, it is against the rules to call a spade a spade ; you must find a stronger name for it, and reserve the comparatively inoffensive "spade" for some such mild implement as a teaspoon. This is among Aristide's numerous dainty methods of certifying his scorn for the shifty refinements of modern life ; and besides, for reasons that are not obvious, he thinks it's funny, and expects people to laugh. So, when presently he

swaggered up to our little group of peace-
able art-students, slapping our shoulders
with violent good-fellowship, he must needs
hail us as *mes mufles, mes cochons, et cetera ;*
and we of course had to approve ourselves
no milksops by smiling delightedly. Then
he lowered his voice, and told us he was in
great distress.

"I've no piano-banger. The cut-purse
who usually does for me has sent word that
he's laid up. Any of these chits here know
how to thump the ivories ?"—chits being
rather a liberal translation of the term that
he employed.

"Chit yourself!" cried Zélie, playfully.
"*Vieux chien!*"

"Can you play the piano?" Chalks asked
in English of Mademoiselle Miss. "Bruant
wants somebody to play his accompani-
ments."

"I can play a little. I could try," she
answered simply.

And Bruant led her to the instrument,

where she sat with her back to the company, and worked hard for its entertainment, till, in about an hour, the delinquent pianist turned up, apparently recovered from his indisposition, and took her place.

Now what were we to make of this ? A young woman going to Bruant's (than which there is scarcely a shadier resort in all the shady by-ways of Bohemia)—going to Bruant's for the first time in her life, boldly gets up, and takes part in the performance ! How were we to penetrate beneath the surface of her conduct, and perceive the world of innocence, the supreme unconsciousness of evil, that lay hidden there, and accounted for it ?   Bruant himself, to our shame be it owned,—rough, ribald, rowdy Aristide,— saw what we were blind to.

"How the devil does *she* come to be knocking about with your flash mob ? " he asked me, in the pauses of one of his songs ; he struts hither and thither through the room, as he sings, you know and exchanges

parenthetical remarks with everybody.
"You're no fit pals for the likes of her,
vous autres, *b*——, *m*—— *!*"—words that
would put any English printing-machinery
out of gear.

"Why not?" I queried meekly.

"Because she's an honest girl, that's all.
She's fallen among thieves, and I believe she
doesn't know it. You oughtn't to have
brought her to a *sale trou* like this."

"I didn't bring her. She came of her own
free will."

"Well, it's some ridiculous mistake, mark
what I'm telling you." And he moved off
singing the second stanza of "Saint Lazare."

Upon the arrival of his own paid pianist,
he conducted Miss back to her seat at our
table, made her a grand bow, thanked her
in a speech every word of which could have
been found in the Academy Dictionary, and
insisted upon her drinking a *galopin* of beer
with him, and clinking glasses. She laughed

and blushed a good deal; but it was plain that in her heart she was murmuring, " What fun ! "

Afterwards we went to the Rat Mort for supper. Yes, heaven forgive us, we took Mademoiselle Miss to the Rat Mort for supper !

One thing, in recalling those early days, I catch myself perpetually thanking our stars for, with a joy the obverse of a terror ; and that is that it was mercifully given to us to find her out before she had a chance to do the same by us. Otherwise,—if we had persisted a little longer in our error, and in our consequent modes of speech and conduct, and she had come to understand,—my heart quails to picture the hurt and mortification she would have suffered, the contempt and horror she must have felt for us. But, by a good fortune that we had certainly done nothing to deserve, our eyes were opened to her true colours in the very nick of time ; and we made haste to turn over a

new leaf before she had been able to spell
out the old. I can hardly tell just how it
began. It began probably in vague misgiv-
ings, dim surmises, that gradually waxed
stronger and clearer, and were in the end
confirmed by circumstances. Little questions she would ask, little comments she
would make, little things she would do,
struck us as odd, as hopeless to explain,—
unless on an hypothesis that at first seemed
quite too far-fetched, but by-and-by forced
itself upon us as the only one that would
in any way fit the case ; the hypothesis,
namely, of her stupendous innocence ; that,
indeed, as Bruant had divined, her presence
with us was due to some preposterous miscon-
ception ; that, in her own perfect soundness
and honesty, she was totally unsuspicious of
the corruption round about her.

Chalks used to give expression to this
growing sentiment of ours, by shaking his
head, looking half wise, half mystified, and
muttering, ''There's something queer about

that girl. I'll be gol-donged if I can make her out."

Once for instance, she confided to us that she thought Madame Bourdon must be a very religious person, because she was always with a priest. It was clear that she proffered this remark in entire literalness and good faith, with no ulterior intention of any sort; and we, after staring at it for a minute or two, reflected upon it for a fortnight. True enough, the black robe of Monsieur the Abbé did lend a meretricious air of orthodoxy both to Madame and to her establishment.

Then the fact came out, I can't remember how, that she was working at Julian's, —taking "whole days," too, which means nine or ten hours of heavy labour in the pestilential air of a studio packed with people, where every window is shut, and the temperature hovers between eighty and ninety Fahrenheit. Why should she be breaking her back and poisoning her lungs at Julian's, if——?

" There's something queer about her," Chalks insisted.

She was always extremely friendly, though, with the other ladies of our household : visited them in their rooms, received them in her own, walked out with them, chatted with them as freely as her French would let her ; and this confused us, and deferred our better judgment. It was hard to believe that anybody, no matter how guileless, nor how ill-instructed in their idiom, could rub elbows much with Zélie, Yvonne, Fifine, and not become more or less distinctly aware of the peculiarities of their temperament. If actions speak louder than words, manners nowadays are masters of seven languages.

Yet, one afternoon, in the garden of the Luxembourg, Miss asked of me, " Are they all married, those young ladies at our hotel ? "

3

I looked at her for a moment in a sort of stupefaction. Was it her pleasure to be jocular? No, she had spoken in utmost sobriety.

"Married?" I echoed. "What on earth made you think they're married?"

"Everybody calls them Madame. I thought in French Madame was only used for married women, like Mrs. with us."

Some providential instinct in me bade me respect her simplicity, and answer with a prevarication.

"Oh, no," I said, "not in the Latin Quarter, at any rate. It's the custom here to call all women Madame."

"But then," she proceeded with swift logic, "why do they call me Mademoiselle?"

This was rather a "oner," but I came up manfully. "Ah, that's—that's because you're English, don't you see?"

"Oh," she murmured, apparently accepting the reason as sufficient.

Then I ventured to sound her a little.

"You like them, you find them pleasant, the girls at the hotel?"

"Yes, I like them," she answered deliberately. "Of course, their ways aren't quite English, are they? But I suppose one must expect French girls to be different. They seem intelligent and good-natured, and they've been very nice to me."

"I dare say you don't always understand each other?" I suggested.

"Oh dear no. That is what prevents our being intimate. French is so difficult, and they talk so fast. It's as much as I can do to understand the masters at the school, though they speak very slowly and clearly, because they know I'm English. But I think I'm learning a little. I can understand a great deal more than I could when I first came. Do all French girls smoke cigarettes? I knew that Spanish and Russian women did, but I didn't know it was the custom in France."

"Yes, decidedly," I said to myself,

"Chalks is right. There's something 'queer,' about her."

But how to reconcile the theory of her "queerness" with the fact of her residence here alone among us in the Latin Quarter of Paris ? Assuming her to be a well brought-up, innocent young English girl, how in the name of verisimilitude had she con-trived to get so far astray from her natural orbit ?

Nevertheless, in the teeth of difficulties, the theory gained ground. And as it did so, it was amusing to note the way in which the other girls accepted it. They were thor-oughly scandalized, poor dears. Their sense of propriety bridled up in indignant aston-ishment. So long as they had been able to reckon Miss, simply and homogeneously, a case of total depravity,—a specimen of the British variety of their own species,—they had placed no stint upon their affable com-mendation of her. She was *pas mal, très bien, très gentille, très comme il faut,* even *très chic.* But directly the suspicion began to work in their minds that perhaps, after all, appearances had been misleading, and she might prove an entirely vertical member of society,—then perforce they had to wag their heads over her, and cry fie at her goings-on. What! how! a respectable unmarried woman,—a *demoiselle du monde,*—a *jeune fille bien élevée,*—come by herself to Paris,—dwell unchaperoned in the Hôtel de l'Océan et de Shakespere,—hob and nob familiarly with you and me,—submit to be *tutoyée* by Tom, Dick, and Harry! *Mais, allons donc,* it was really quite too shameless. And they played my ladies Steyne and Bareacres to her inadequate Rebecca ; looked askance at her when she came into the room, drew in their precious skirts when they had to pass her, gathered in corners to discuss her, and were, in fine, profoundly and sincerely shocked. For, here below, there are no sterner moralists, no more punctilious sticklers for the prunes and prisms of conventionality, than those harmful, unnecessary cats, the Zélies and the Germaines of the *Quartier-Latin.*

"*Mais, enfin, si c'est vrai,—si elle est réellement comme ça, n'est-ce pas,—mais c'est une honte,*" was one of their refrains ; and "*Elle manque complètement de pudeur alors,*" was another ; to which the chorus : "*Oh, pour sûr !*"

And poor little Miss couldn't understand it. Observing the frigid and austere reserve with which they met her, feeling their half suppressed disapproval in the atmosphere, she searched her conscience vainly to discover what she could have done to anger them, and was, for a time, I fear, exceedingly unhappy.

We men, meanwhile, were cursing our· selves for blockheads, chewing the sharp cud of repentance, and trying in a hundred sheepish, clumsy fashions to make amends. It would have been diverting for an outsider to have watched us ; the deference with which we spoke and listened to her, the in-

terest we took in her work, the infinite little
politenesses we paid her. When all is said,
the sins we were guilty of towards her had
been chiefly metaphysical ; it was what we
had thought, rather than what we had done.
But I don't know that our contrition was on
this account any the less acute; we had
thought such a lot. We fancied a sister of
our own in her position, and we conceived
a frantic desire to punch the heads of the
men who should have dared to think of
her as we, quite nonchalantly and with no
sense of daring, had thought of Miss. Our
biggest positive transgression was the lati-
tude of speech we had allowed ourselves at
the table d'hôte ; and the effect of that was
happily neutralised (no thanks to us) by the
poverty of her French. But, though our
salvation lay in the circumstance, I am far
from sure that it did not aggravate our remorse. We were profiting by her limitations,
taking sanctuary in her ignorance ; and that
smacked disagreeably of the sneakish.

Our yearning to make amends was singularly complicated by the necessity we were
under, as much for her sake as for our own,
to prevent her ever guessing how (or even
that) we had offended.   Not to confess is to
shirk the better half of atonement ; yet confession in this case was impossible, conceal-
ment was imperative.   That, if she should
get so much as a glimmer of the truth, it would
blast us forever in her esteem, was a consideration, but a trifling one to the thought of
what her emotions must be like to realise the
sort of place she had lately held in ours.
No, she must never guess.   With the con-
sciousness in our hearts that we had practised a kind of intellectual foul play upon
her, and in our minds a vivid picture of the
different footing things would be on if she
only knew, we must continue cheerfully to
enjoy her smiles and her good graces, and
try to look as if we felt that we deserved
them.   It was bare-faced hypocrisy, it was
a game of false pretences ; but it was Hob-

son's choice. We could not even cease to thee-and-thou her, lest she should wonder at the change, and from wonderment proceed to ratiocination.

"One thing we must do, though," said Chalks, "we must get her out of this so-called hotel. Blamed if I can guess how she ever came here."

This was before we had found the guide-book in her room, long before we had heard her simple story, which explained every-thing.

"We've acted like a pack of hounds, that's my opinion," Chalks went on. "And now we've got to step up to the captain's office and settle."

His rhetoric was confused, but I dare say we caught the idea.

"We've been acting like a pack of poodles latterly," somebody put in, "following her about, fawning at her feet, fetching and carrying for her."

"Well, and hadn't we oughter?" de-

manded Chalks. "Is there any gentleman here who doesn't like it?"

"Oh, no, I only mentioned the circumstance as a source of unction," said the
speaker.

"Chalks is right. We must get her out of
the hotel," Campbell agreed. "She mustn't
be exposed any longer to contact with those
little beasts of Mimis."

"That's all very well, but how are we to
manage it?" inquired Norton. "We can't
give her the word to move, without saying
why. And as I understand it, that's precisely the last thing we wish to do."

"We want to get her out of the mud,
without letting her know she's in it," said
another.

"Yes, that's the devil of it," admitted
Chalks. "But I'll tell you what," he added,
with an air of inspiration. "Why not work
it from the other end round? Get rid of the
Mimis, and let Miss stop?"

This proposition was so radical, so revo-

lutionary, we were inclined to greet it with
derision. But Chalks stood by his guns.

"How to do it?" he cried. "Why, boy-
cott 'em. Make this shop too hot to hold
'em. Cultivate the art of being infernally
disagreeable. They'll clear out fast enough.
Then there'd be no harm in Miss staying till
the end of time."

"What'll Madame say?"

"Oh, we can fill their places up with fel-
lows. I'll go touting among the men at
the school. Easy enough to bag a half a
dozen."

"But what about Lucile?"—Lucile, it will
be remembered, was Madame's niece.

"That's so," confessed Chalks, dashed for
a moment. "Lucile's the snag. But I guess
on the whole Lucile will have to go too.
I'll hire a man I know to want her room.
Madame won't let family feeling stand in
the way of trade. Especially the sky-pilot
won't, not he. And I'd like to know who's
the boss of this shebang, if not Monsieur the

Abbé? There's no love lying around loose between him and Lucile, as it stands. Just let a man turn up and ask for her room, Madame'll drop her like a hot potato."

But from the labour of putting such schemes in operation we were saved by a microbe: a mouse can serve a lion. Half of our male contingent went down with the influenza: and our ladies, Lucile included, incontinently fled the ship. They dreaded the infection; and the house was as melancholy as a hospital; and noise being inhibited, they couldn't properly entertain their friends. Besides, I think they were glad enough of an occasion to escape from the proximity of Miss. She had infused an element of ozone into our moral atmosphere; their systems weren't accustomed to it; it filled them with a vague *malaise*: they made a break for fouler air.

And it was at this crisis that Miss came out strong. She laid aside all business and excuses, and constituted herself our nurse.

All day long, and very nearly all night long
too, she was at it : flying from room to room,
administering medicines to this man, reading
aloud to that, spraying eucalyptus everywhere, running for the doctor when somebody appeared to have taken a turn for the
worse,—in short, heaping coals of fire upon
our heads with a lavish, untiring hand.
When we got up from our sick-beds, every
mother's son of us was dead in love with her.
From that time to the end she went about
like a queen with her body-guard ; and there
wasn't one of us who wouldn't have given
his life to spare her a pain in the little finger ;
and our rewards were her smiles. It is to
be noted that she accepted our devotion
with the same calm unconsciousness of anything extraordinary that she had shown in the
old days to our doubtful courtesy. She wore
her crown and wielded her gentle sceptre
like one in the purple born, whilst her subjects outdid each other in zeal to please her.

Meantime we had learned her previous

history ; we had pieced it together from a multitude of little casual utterances. Her father, some five years ago, had died a bankrupt ; and she had gone as governess with an English family to the far West of America, where they had a cattle ranch ; and now she was on her way home, to seek a new engagement ; and she was breaking her pilgrimage with a season of art in Paris (she had always wanted to cultivate her natural gift for painting) ; and she had chosen the Hôtel de l'Océan et de Shakespere because her guide-book recommended it.

Now Norton had a sister married to a squire in Derbyshire ; and one day this good lady advertised in the *Times* for a governess ; and Miss, who kept watch on such advertisements (going to Neal's library to study the English papers), was on the point of answering it, when Norton cut in with a "Let me write that letter for you. Mrs. Clere happens to be my sister." Of course Miss got the place ; and it was to take it, and begin her duties, that she left us last night.

I follow her in fancy upon her journey, and imagine her arrival at the big, respectable, dull country house ; and I wonder will she regret a little and think fondly now and then of Madame Bourdon's hotel and the ragged staff of comrades she has left behind her here. For the present the Rue Racine is an abhorrent vacuum, and I am sick with nostagia for the Paris of yesterday.

THE FUNERAL MARCH OF A MARIONNETTE

" Elle est morte et n'a point vécu."

WHO does not know the sensation that
besets an ordinary man on entering a familiar room, where, during his absence, some
change has been made?—a piece of furni-
ture moved, an old hanging taken down, a
new picture put up?—that teasing sense
of strangeness, which, if subordinate to the
business of the moment, yet persists, uncom-
fortably formless, till, for instance, the pre-
siding genius of the place inquires, "How
do you like the way we have moved the
piano?" or something else happens to crys-
tallise the sufferer's mere vague feeling into

a perception ; after which his spirit may be at rest again ?

When I woke this morning, here in my own dingy furnished room, in this most dingy lodging-house, I had an experience very like that I mean to suggest : something seemed wrong and unusual, something had been changed overnight. This was the more perplexing, because my door had remained locked and bolted ever since I had tucked myself into bed ; and *within* the room, after all, there isn't much to change ; only the bed itself, and the armoire, and my writing-table, and my wash-hand-stand, and my two dilapidated chairs ; and these were still where they belonged. So were the shabby green window-curtains, the bilious green paper on the walls, the dismal green baldaquin above my head. Nevertheless, a tantalising sense of something changed, of something taken away, of an unwonted vacancy, haunted me through the brewing and the drinking of my coffee, and through

the first few whiffs of my cigarette. Then
I put on my hat, and " went to school," and
forgot about it.

But when I came back, in the afternoon,
I found that whatever the cause might be
of my curious psychical disturbance, it had
not ceased to act. No sooner had I got
seated at my table, and begun to arrange
my notes, than down upon me settled,
stronger if possible than ever, that inexpli-
cable feeling of emptiness in the room, of
strangeness, of an accustomed something
gone. What could it mean? It was dis-
quieting, exasperating ; it interfered with
my work. I must investigate it, and put an
end to it, if I could.

But just at that moment the current of my
ideas was temporarily turned by somebody
rapping on my door. I called out, "*Entrez !*"
and there entered a young lady : a young
lady in black, with soiled yellow ribbons,
and on her cheeks a little artificial bloom.
The effect of this, however, was mitigated

by a series of flesh-colored ridges running through it ; and as the young person's eyes, moreover, were red and humid, I concluded that she had been shedding tears.   I looked at her for two or three seconds without being able to think who she was ; but before she had pronounced her "*B' jour, monsieur,*" I remembered : Madame Germaine, the friend of poor little Zizi, my next-door neighbour.   And then, in a flash, the reason appeared to me for my queer dim feeling of something not as usual in my surroundings, *I had not heard Zizi cough !*   That was it ! Zizi, the poor little girl in the adjoining room,—behind that door against which my armoire stands,—who for three months past has scarcely left the house, but has coughed, coughed, coughed perpetually : so that every night I have fallen asleep, and every morning wakened, and every day pursued my indoor occupations, to that distressing sound.   Oh, our life is not all cakes and ale, here in the Quarter ; we have

our ennuis, as well as the rest of mankind;
and when we are too poor to change our
lodgings, we must be content to abide in
patience—whatever sounds our neighbours
choose to make.

At all events, so it came to pass that the
sight of Madame Germaine, in her soiled
finery, cleared up my problem for me: Zizi
had not coughed. And I said to myself,
"Ah, the poor little thing is better, and is
spending the day out of doors." (It has been
a lovely day, soft as April, though in mid-
winter; and my inference, therefore, was
not overdrawn.) "And Madame Germaine,"
I proceeded rapidly, "has come to see her;
and finding her away, has looked in on
me."

Meanwhile my visitor stood still, just
within the threshold, and gazed solemnly,
almost reproachfully, at me with her big
protruding eyes : eyes that, protruding always far more than enough, seemed now,
swollen by recent weeping, fairly ready to

leave their sockets. What had she been crying for, I wondered.

Then I began our conversation with a cheery "Zizi isn't there?"

"*Ah, m'sieu! Ah, la pauv' Zizi!*" was her response, in a sort of hysterical gasp; and two fresh tears rolled down her cheeks, making further havoc of her rouge. She took a few steps forward, and sank into my arm-chair. "*La pauv' petite!*" she sobbed.

I was puzzled, of course, and a little troubled. "What is it? What is the matter?" I asked. "Zizi isn't worse, surely? I haven't heard her cough all day."

"Oh, no, *m'sieu*, she isn't worse. Oh, no, she—she is dead."

I don't need to recount any more of my interview with Madame Germaine, though it lasted a good half-hour longer, and was sufficiently vivacious. I can't describe to you the shock her announcement caused me, nor the chill and despondency that have been growing on me ever since. Zizi—

dead ? Zizi and Death !—the notions are too awfully incongruous. I look at the door that separates our rooms,—the door athwart which, in former times, I have heard so many bursts of laughter, snatches of song, when Zizi would be entertaining her. . . . . she called them "friends ; " and, latterly, that hacking, unyielding cough of hers,—I look at the door, and a sort of cold and blackness seems to creep in from its edges ; and then I fancy the darkened chamber beyond it, with the open window, and Zizi's little form stretched on the bed, stark and dead,—poor little chirping, chattering, ribald Zizi ! Oh, it is ghastly. And all her trumpery, twopenny fripperies round about her, their occupation gone : her sham jewels, and her flounces, and her tawdry furs and laces, and her powder-puffs and rouge-pots —though it was only towards the end that Zizi took to rouge. It is as if they were to tell you that a *doll* is dead : can such things *die ?* They are not wholly inhuman, then ?

They have viscera? are made of real flesh
and blood? can experience real pains? and
—and die? Here are you and I, serious
folk, not without some sense of the solem-
nity and mystery of God's creation, here are
we still working the first degree of our
arcana,—Life; and yonder lies that tinselled
little gewgaw, admitted to the second! She
has passed the dread portals, she has accomplished the miracle of Death! She was
vain and shallow and hard: she was mali-
cious: she was shameless in her speech as
in her conduct: she was lively, it is true,
and merry-mannered, and pretty: but she
had no affections, no illusions, no remorse;
and lies dropped like toads from her mouth
whenever she opened it: yet she is dead!
And to-morrow women (who would have
shrunk from her in her lifetime, as from
something pestilential) will reverently cross
themselves, and men (who would have. . . .
ah, well, it is best not to remember what
the men would have done) will decently

bare their heads, as her poor coffin is borne through the streets on its way to the grave-yard. Isn't it ghastly? Isn't it quite enough to depress a fellow, to sober him up, when there is only a thin partition, broken by a door, to separate him from such a death-chamber?—Wait ; I must tell you something about Zizi, as I have known her.

Long before our personal acquaintance began I used to see her here and there in the Quarter : at the Bullier balls, or the Café Vachette, or in the Luxembourg or the Boule-Miche when the weather was fine : and to admire her as a singularly inoffensive speci-men of her class. Those were her palmy days. Her "friend" was a student of law, from the Quartier Marbœuf, with a pocketful of money and a pointed beard. She was the smallest of possible little women, no higher than her law-student's heart, if he had one ; and he was only a medium-sized Frenchman. She was very daintily formed, with fine hands and feet ; she had a great quantity of black hair, and a pair of bright black eyes. Her face was pale, and decidedly an interesting face: pert, if you please, and tremendously mischievous, but suggestive of wit, of intelligence, even of humour and passion: a most uncommon face, with character in it,—I believe I may even say with distinction. It was a face you would have noticed anywhere, to wonder who and what its owner might be. And then she used to dress very well, very quietly: in refined grays or blacks: there was absolutely nothing in her dress to betray her place in the world's economy: passing her in the street, you would have taken her for an entirely irreproachable little housewife, with an unusually interesting face. I used to see her in all the pleasure-resorts of the Quarter, and to admire her, and speculate about her in a languid, melancholy way. Then I left town for the summer; and when I came back last September I established myself here in the Hôtel du Saint Esprit.

The first morning after my arrival I was awakened by queer but unambiguous noises coming through that door, there behind my armoire ; a strident laugh, and a few hardy exclamations, that could leave me in no doubt as to the sex and quality of my fellow-lodger. An hour or two later I encountered Zizi on the landing; and the concierge informed me that she was the tenant of the next room to my own. Such a neighbourship would horrify you in London or New York: but we think nothing of accidents much worse than that, here in the Latin Quarter of Paris. Afterwards, night and morning, and more especially in those small hours that are properly both or neither, I would hear Zizi's laughter beyond our dividing door ; her laughter, or her thin little voice raised in a stupid song, or the murmur of light talk, that would sometimes leap to the pitch of anger, for I suspect that Zizi's temper was uncertain ; and then, rare at first, but recurring more and more frequently, till it became quite the dominant note, her hard, dry, racking little cough.

Elinor was in Paris about this time. To my great joy, she had come to pass the autumn, and perhaps the winter too; and she was very anxious that I should show her something of the seamy side of life here. She had taken lodgings on the other—the right and wrong—bank of the river; and every afternoon, my day's work done, I would join her there, and we would go off together for little excursions into Bohemia. I happened to be extraordinarily flush for the moment; I had nearly two hundred pounds of ready money; and this was a help. Of course I took her to the Moulin Rouge, which disgusted her, as I had warned her that it would; and to the Chat Noir, which amused her; and I was fortunate enough to get two seats for a performance at the Théâtre Libre, which both amused and disgusted her at once; and I introduced her to the jerry-built splendours of Bullier;

and we took long delightful walks together
in the Luxembourg, where she would feed the
sparrows with crumbs of unnutritious bread ;
and we lunched, dined, and supped together
in an infinite number of droll restaurants ;
and now and then we went slumming in
the far north, or east, or south ; and Pousset's
knew us, and Vachette's ; and sometimes,'
for the fun or the convenience of the thing,
we would drop in among the *demi-gomme*
of the Café de la Paix : and she would have
been altogether happy and contented save
for a single unfulfilled desire. She wanted
to make acquaintance with some member
of the sisterhood of *Sainte Griselle ;* she
wanted, as a literary woman, to see what
such an one would be like ; to convince herself whether or not they were as black as
I had painted them, for I had painted them
very black indeed.

"Well," I said at last, "you'll be sorry
for it, but since you won't take no for an
answer, I'll see what can be done."

Then one afternoon I was waiting for her by appointment, in that very Café de la Paix, when whom should I see enter, and ensconce themselves in a back room, but my neighbour Zizi, and her friend of the ribbons, Madame Germaine.   " When Elinor arrives," I thought, "and if her heart is still set on that sort of thing, I will introduce Zizi to her : for Zizi is as nearly innocuous as a microbe of her variety very well can be." Elinor arrived a moment later : beautiful, strong, gracious, and pure as a May morning : and I proposed the measure to her; and her instant decision was, "Oh, yes, by all means." So she and I penetrated into the back room, and took the table next to Zizi's ; and presently Zizi gave me a sly little covert glance and smile ; and therewith I invited her and her companion to come and sit with us.

"Madame permits ? " demanded Zizi, raising her eyebrows, astonished at such magnanimity on the part of a fellow-woman. Elinor smiled assent ; and the two *étudiantes* rose and placed themselves before our own slab of marble. I asked them what they would take; of course they commanded each a *menthe à l'eau*. But though I tried to suit the conversation to their taste and level, they were not perfectly at ease. The presence of Elinor, whom, for all that she was alone with a man in the Café de la Paix, they could perceive with half an eye to be a bird of a totally different feather to their own, embarrassed them a good deal. Their desire to appear well before her, their determined best behaviour, tied their tongues, and made them surpassingly dull; for when they are not flavoured lavishly with Gallic salt, they are unimaginably insipid, these little soubrettes in the comedy of evil. However, before we broke up, I had engaged them to breakfast with us on the Sunday to follow. We were all to meet at Pousset's in the Boulevard at noon, and thence we would proceed to the Abbaye de Thélème, where I would bespeak a *cabinet particulier.*

The Abbaye de Thélème is the riskiest of restaurants in a most risky quarter : but Elinor wanted to see the seamy side of Parisian life, and I was resolved to satisfy her once for all with a drastic measure of it.

" *Voyez-vous,*" I heard Zizi boasting to her, in a whisper, "it is forbidden for women to come alone to this café. But I am an honest girl. The *gérant* knows me. They make no objection to me or to my friends. *Adieu, madame. Au revoir, proche,*"—this last to me. *Proche,* indeed! But in the Latin Quarter the word is often used as a substitute for *voisin.* Then Zizi took her small self off, followed by Germaine.

"Well," I queried, as soon as Elinor and I were alone, "is your thirst for experience satisfied ? Are you happy at last ? "

" I am overcome with bewilderment. Who would have known that they weren't simply two ordinary bourgeoises ? There wasn't anything rowdy or shocking about them."

" What ! The rouge ? The ribbons ? The bulging eyes?"

"Oh, I wasn't thinking of that one. I didn't care much for her. Still, even she looked no worse than—well, a shop-girl. But the other, the little one. I shouldn't have been surprised to meet her anywhere, —at Madame X——'s, at Madame de Z——'s. She was dressed so quietly, in such good taste. Her manners were so subdued, almost English. And her face,—it's a face that would strike you anywhere. So delicate, refined, so quaint and interesting. *She* doesn't rouge. And such lovely hair ! Oh, I am sure she is full of good qualities. What a shame and horror it is that . . . that. . . It makes one feel inclined to loathe your whole sex." Elinor's commentary at this point became a lamentation, which it would be irrelevant to repeat. "I must get her to tell me her story," was its conclusion.

"Oh, she'll tell you her story fast enough, only, I warn you, it will be a pack of

5

lies.   The truth isn't in them, those little puppets.   Don't cherish any illusions about her.   The most one can say for her is that she's a fairly harmless example of a desperately bad class.   The grisette of Musset, of Henry Murger, exists no longer, even if she ever did exist.   To-day Zizi was on her good behaviour.   Sunday, I hope for the sake of science, she'll get off it, and be her wicked little self.   Yes, her face is remarkable, but it's an absurd accident, a slip of nature : not one of the qualities it would seem to indicate is anywhere in her— neither wit nor humour nor emotion.   She's just a little undersized cat; not a kitten : she has none of the innocent gentleness of a kitten : an undergrown, hard, sprightly little cat.   However, she can be amusing enough when she's roused; and on Sunday we are likely to have a merry breakfast."

But herein I proved myself a false prophet. We were still at the *hors d'œuvres* when Zizi began to cry.   She had coughed ; and Elinor

had asked her if she had a cold ; and that
question precipitated a flood of tears. This
was dispiriting. It is always dispiriting to
see one of these creatures anything but gay
and flippant : serious feeling is so crudely,
so garishly, at variance with your preconcep-
tion of them, with the mood in which you
approach them. And yet they cry a good
deal,—mostly, however, tears of mere spite
or vexed vanity ; or, it may be, of hysteria,
for they are frightfully subject to what they
call *crises de nerfs*. But Zizi's tears now
were of a different water. Had she a cold ?
Oh, no, it was worse than that. The doctor
said her lungs were affected ; and if she
didn't speedily change her mode of life, she
must go into a decline. And this, if you
please, was the dish laid on our table, there
in the vulgar *cabinet particulier* of that shady
restaurant, under the crystal gasalier, and
between the four diamond-scratched looking-
glasses that covered the walls,—this was
the dish served to us even before the oysters ;

and you may imagine, therefore, with what
appetite we attacked the good things that
came after.   The doctor had told her that
she must absolutely suspend her dissipations for at least a six-month, and rest, and
soigner herself, and "feed up," or she would
surely become *poitrinaire.*   "And do nothing? How can I? *Faut vivre, parbleu!*"   Her
present friend-in-chief, she explained, was
at the School of Mines ; his pension from
his family only amounted to two hundred
and fifty francs a month ; he was all that is
good, he would do his utmost for her ; but
she couldn't live on what he could spare
her out of two hundred and fifty francs a
month.

With this she went off in a regular fit of hysterics ; and Elinor had her hands full, trying to
bring her round.   Hysterics are infectious ; and
Madame Germaine sat in her place, and sobbed
helplessly,—not in sympathy, but by infection,
—whilst her tears fell into her plate.

I saw that Elinor was tremendously dis-
tressed, and I cursed the misinspired moment
when I had arranged this feast. "Terrible,
terrible!" she murmured, shaking her head
and looking at me with pained eyes. When
at length Zizi was calm again, Elinor asked,
"You won't mind if I speak with Monsieur
in English?" and then said to me, "This
is quite too dreadful. We must do something for her. We must save her from con-
sumption; and perhaps at the same time
we can redeem her, make a good woman
of her. She has it in her."

I respected Elinor's sincerity too much to
laugh at the utopian quality of her optimism :
so I waived the latter of her remarks, and
replied only to the former. "I should be
glad to do anything possible for her, but I
don't exactly see what *is* possible. Besides,
I don't believe she's threatened with con-
sumption, any more than I am. This is a
pose, to make herself interestingly pathetic
in your eyes, and get some money. You'll

see—she's going to strike me for fifty francs. It's the sum they usually ask for. And she wants to win your sanction to the gift beforehand."

Surely enough, Zizi lifted up her tearful face, its features all puffed out and empurpled, and said at this very moment, in a whimper that ought to have hardened the softest heart, "If Monsieur could give me a little money--a couple of louis—a fifty-franc note? I could buy medicines and things."

"Nonsense," said I, brutally; "you'd buy *chiffons* and things."

She laughed without offence, and gave me a knowing glance, but protested, "*Non, sérieusement, je veux me soigner.*" Then she turned to Elinor, and pleaded coaxingly, "Madame, tell him to give me fifty francs— *pour me soigner.*"

"No," Elinor replied; "he won't give you fifty francs, but this is what he *will* do, what *we* will do. If you will obey the doctor's orders, send your friends about their business, and lead a perfectly regular life for the time being, we will undertake to see that you want for nothing during the next six months. After that, *nous verrons !* For the present, that is what we offer you : six months in which to give yourself every chance for a cure. Only, during those six months—*faut être sage.*"

Of course, Zizi began to cry again ; and, of course, she could do nothing less than accept Madame's proposition with some show of effusion : though I mistrusted the whole-heartedness of her acceptance ; she would much rather have pocketed the fifty francs, and had done with us.

Elinor and she fell to discussing sundry practical details. Good and abundant food, warm clothing, healthful lodgings : these were the three desiderata that Elinor pre-scribed. As for the last, Zizi assured us that she already had them—"since I live in the same house as Monsieur," she explained, convincingly.

But Elinor was not convinced. "Do your rooms face south?" was the question she insisted on.

Now Zizi, about the points of the compass, and such abstruse matters generally, had no more idea than I have of Sanskrit; yet, "Oh, yes, my room gives to the noon," she answered, without turning a hair. "And, anyhow, it is a very nice room.—Come and see," she added, impulsively. "I should be charmed to show you."

"I suppose it will be all right?" Elinor asked of me.

"Oh, no worse than the rest," I acquiesced.

And so we took a cab, and were driven to the Rue St. Jacques. Madame Germaine parted from us at the threshold of the eating-house. "I have an engagement in the Parc Monceau," she informed us, in the candour of her heart. Zizi jeered at her a good deal as we drove across the town. " Her ribbons— *hein ?* Her goggle-eyes! Not at all *comme il faut.* But a brave girl. She loves me like a sister. Monsieur smiles. No, word of honour, it is not as you think." If I had thought as Zizi thought I thought, I shouldn't have smiled ; but she, of course, couldn't be expected to understand that. "Poor Germaine ! Her real name is Gobbeau, Marthe Gobbeau. She is stupid and ugly, but she is good-natured," which was more, perhaps, than one could say with truth of her little critic. "Her mother is an *ouvreuse* in the Théâtre de Belleville."

"And her father ? " queried Elinor.

"Her father ! " cried Zizi, and she was about to continue, when it occurred to her to respect Elinor's unsophistication. She gave me a furtive wink, and said, gravely, "Oh, her father lives in the twenty-first arrondissement." Elinor was not aware that the arrondissements of Paris number only twenty, and so she could not realise either the double meaning or the antiquity of this evasion.

Zizi's room was precisely like a thousand other rooms in the Latin Quarter, though rather more luxurious than most : much more so than mine, for example. To begin with, she had a carpet, her private property, a sober-hued Brussels carpet, that covered almost the entire floor ; then she had four chairs, each practicable and reasonably fresh-looking ; her bed was enriched by a counter-pane of crimson silk, and crimson too were the hangings over it. The walls were deco-rated in the prevailing style of her class and epoch, with tambourines, toy trumpets, empty bonbon boxes, and so forth, hung from tin-tacks. But the chief impression that you got of the room was one of clean-liness and order : Zizi, still for all slips of hers, was French.

"How very neat it is, how exquisitely neat," Elinor murmured, in evident sur-prise.

Zizi smiled complacently,—with what they call proper pride. "*Pas mal, hein ? Assez chic, eh ?*" she questioned, whilst her eyes snapped triumphantly.

"Yes," Elinor admitted, "it is very nice, but—it looks due north."

And she proceeded to develop her favourite hygienic thesis, to the effect that no one could keep well who lived in a room that had no sun, the application being that Zizi must change her quarters. To-morrow, Monday, she must find a room that really did "give to the noon ;" and at three o'clock we would meet her at the Vachette, and go with her to inspect it. Of course we were to pay the rent.

"My dear Elinor," I said, when we had taken leave of Zizi, "I am sorry to discourage you, but your benevolent schemes will come to nothing. She won't change her lodgings, and she won't change her mode of life. We would much better have given her a little ready cash, and got rid of her. An endeavour to be respectable, if only *ad interim* as it were, would weary her too much.

You rashly promised to see that she wanted for nothing. Can you see that she has plenty of excitement?—which is the breath of her nostrils. To-morrow she will draw back; she will tell you that on the whole she finds she can't accept your bigger offer, and will renew her request for fifty francs."

"If I didn't know you weren't, I should think you were a perfectly soulless cynic," was Elinor's rejoinder.

But, cynic or no cynic, I was right. Elinor, in agreeing to meet Zizi at Vachette's on the morrow, had forgotten a previous engagement, which she remembered afterwards; so I went to the rendezvous alone, charged, however, with full powers to act as I might deem best. Zizi was a quarter-hour late, but she didn't mind that, apparently; at any rate she vouchsafed no apology for having kept me waiting. She made haste to let me know that she couldn't possibly change her lodgings; she hadn't even looked for others : her mother wouldn't hear of it, for one thing; and then—her friends? They all have mothers, somehow or other, though the notion seems incongruous: yet I suppose it's only natural. Zizi's was a purple-faced old *sage femme* from the purlieus of Montmartre. She had taken counsel with her mother, she said, and her mother wouldn't hear of her changing her abode. And then—her friends? When they came to see her, and found that she had moved, they would be displeased; they wouldn't follow her up. Business is business, after all, but in our youth we were taught that friendship isn't. Anyhow, Zizi foresaw herself quite friendless if she moved. "But my room is very well. If you and Madame want to support me, why not support me there?"

I echoed, rather feebly perhaps, Elinor's lecture on the advantages of sunlight; and in any case, I told her, desirous as Madame and I were to "support her," we positively declined to permit ourselves that indulgence, unless she took a sunny room : what we really wished was to help her to get well; we were persuaded that she couldn't get well in a northern aspect ; and we had no sort of eagerness to throw our money from the windows. It was pretty clear to me that she had begun to distrust our motives : such unaccustomed kindness, such reckless extravagance, bore on their face a suspicious look.

"*Et cette dame ?*" she queried.   "*Cette anglaise ? Qu'est-ce qu'elle me veut ? Elle est la maîtresse, hein ? Femme mariée, eh ? Et toi, avec ton petit air Sainte-Nitouche, va !* I'll tell you what : give me some money, fifty francs, to buy medicines, to pay a doctor. Come on !   Fifty francs—it isn't much."

"Yes, it is, my dear," I retorted.   "It's a jolly lot, as you know very well.   But still, if you prefer the part, when you might have the whole, that is your affair ; and so I'm going to give it to you.   Only, mind, this will begin and end the whole transaction.

We give you fifty francs, but we will never give you another penny." Then I smuggled a fifty-franc note into her pretty little hand, —smuggled it, so that the waiters and the other *consommateurs* shouldn't see.

But Zizi was troubled by no such false shame. She smoothed the note out, and held it up to the light, scrutinising it rigorously. Having satisfied herself that it wasn't a counterfeit, she crammed it into a small silver purse, closed the purse with a snap, and buried it in an occult female pocket. At last she turned her face towards mine, and said, "*T'es bon, toi.* That will bring you luck. Kiss me." I suggested that the café was rather too public a place for kissing. The fifty-franc note radiated its genial warmth throughout her small frame, and she quite "chippered up," and laughed and chatted with me very pleasantly. "Why do you never come to see me,—since we live in the same house?" she was good enough to ask. And she tried to pump me, in a naughty insinuating way, about Elinor, her benefactress.

But Zizi was launched upon her descent into Avernus. Her cough got worse and worse ; her cheeks grew hollow, her whole face dragged-looking ; her figure lost its elasticity. She took to rouge and powder, and introduced falsetto notes into her toilet. With her failing health, her friends began to fail her too : coughs and fevers and eyes unnaturally bright are disturbing elements, and put a strain on friendship. She had to seek for new ones, and was to be met with a good deal in the Boulevards. Whenever she spied Elinor and me on her horizon, she bore down upon us, and begged for money : and she was always spying us, always turning up ; it seemed as if she must have dogged our footsteps. Thus you cast your bread upon the waters, and it comes back to you in the fulness of time. She was French, as I have remarked before : but she showed no discretion, and no re-

spect for places or occasions. Not infre-
quently, therefore, her familiar hailings of
us were embarrassing. By and by she ac-
quired a light-hearted habit of entering the
Vachette, ordering what she would, and
leaving it to be scored to my account ; and
I had to remonstrate. At last she found
out Elinor's address, and called upon her.
But Elinor was going to London the next
day ; so nothing came of that. This was in
December ; and early in the same month
Zizi began to keep her room. She was
probably very ill ; she coughed perpetually.
She coughed a good deal when it wasn't
necessary, and only racked without reliev-
ing her poor chest, to say nothing of her
neighbours' nerves. I used to urge her to
control her cough, not to cough when she
could help it ; but self-control of any sort
was beyond her tradition ; and she would
always cough at the slightest impulse.
Once in a great while, if she was a little
better, and the weather favoured, she would

6

put on her rouge and her finery, and go out, —to "*pêcher à la ligne*," as she expressed it. Then, on her re-entrance, I would hear forlorn attempts at song and laughter, which would inevitably end in long, pitiful fits of coughing.

And now it is all over ; Zizi is dead ; and I am as much shocked as if the event were inconsequent and unexpected, as if she hadn't been coughing her life out steadily these three months past. Ah, well, the difficulty is to reconcile one's idea of Zizi with anything not vain and hollow and make-believe, with anything natural and sincere ; and death is so hideously natural, so horribly sincere. For the first time since her birth, I dare say, she has done a sincere thing, a real thing,—she has died !

THE PRODIGAL FATHER.

His wife had died some five and twenty years before, leaving him with an infant son upon his hands ; and she had made him promise that the boy should be brought up as a "good American."

He, poor man, was a desperately bad one. The very word, for instance, as he pronounced it, forgot to rhyme with hurricane ; and, lest anybody should be disposed to look indulgently upon the said offence, I hasten to add that he persistently sounded the *e* in clerk unlike the *i* in dirk. Besides (the homeliness of the detail may be forgiven to its significance), he suffered his nose, as an instrument for the communication of ideas, to sink into disuse and atrophy.

And he lived in London, and brazenly acknowledged that he liked it better than New York.

A serious old friend, writing from oversea to remonstrate with him, spoke of duty and patriotism, and got this pert reply :—

"Duty, my dear, is the last weakness of great minds; and patriotism, as manifested at any rate by such travelling fellow-countrymen of ours as I have met on British soil, patriotism corrupts good manners. Of the patriots themselves I may say, as of divers birds, orators, operas, and women, that they should be seen perhaps, but certainly not heard ; and if I could not talk, I should not wish to live."

As a matter of principle all this rather shocked his young American wife (a Massachusetts girl, who had been bred in the straitest sect of the national religion), though in practice she was nearly as shameless as himself. Anyhow, she submitted cheerfully to a residence in England, and forbore to draw comparisons ; — indeed, if she *had* drawn them, it is not inconceivable that they might have redounded less to the disparagement of the elder country than one could have desired. But then she fell ill, and came to die, and was smitten with home-sickness ; and fond memories of the land of her girlhood begot a sort of dim remorse for the small place she had lately let it hold in her affections ; and groping blindly for something in the nature of atonement, she made her husband promise that the boy should be educated as a good American, in an American school, and at Harvard College.

Afterwards, he transported the baby and its nurse to Beacon Street in Boston, and deposited them with the dead lady's parents. And as soon as he decently could he returned to England; and twenty-five years passed during which neither father nor son crossed the Atlantic.

This I am afraid must be confessed, that

he was a very, very frivolous young person ;
—he carried his age as jauntily as his gloves
and his walking-stick, and would have been
genuinely surprised if anybody had spoken
of him as otherwise than young, though he
was fifty-seven.

With a beggarly five hundred a year to
his patrimony, he lived at the rate of half as
many thousand, he who had never earned a
sixpence.   He had never had time, he said ;
he had been kept too busy doing nothing ;
he had found no leisure for productive industry.   What with teas and dinners and
dances, with visits in country houses and
dashes across the channel, with reading and
conversation, dreaming and sleeping, his
days and nights had been too full ; and so
he had had to raise the balance of his ex-
penditures by leaving the greater number of
his debts unpaid.   For pocket-money he re-
sorted to what he called reversed post-obits.
His son would some day, by inheritance
from his maternal grandparents, be a rich

man ; and he would surely not refuse, on his father's death, to buy up such stamped paper as might bear his father's autograph ; and the Jews (a race that always set great hopes upon posterity) were happy, with this prospect in view, to accommodate him at sixty per cent. per annum.

He was tall and lean and loosely built, much given to lounging about in queer twisted postures, as if double-jointed ; whereby a friend was led to suggest for his consideration that, when hard-up, he might turn an honest penny by enlisting in some itinerant menagerie as India-rubber man. One of his eyes met the world unarmoured, with a perfectly vacant stare ; the other glimmered ambiguously behind a circular shield of glass. He had an odd, musical, rather piping voice, in which he drawled forth absurdities with such a plaintive, weary, spoiled-child intonation as seemed to hint wits tottering and spirits drooping under an almost insupportable burden of fatigue and disappointment ; whence, for a stranger, it was not at once easy to determine if his utterances were funny or only inconsequential. When I first made his acquaintance, I remember, I thought for a minute or two that I had stumbled upon a tired imbecile, —then an amusing one,—then an inspired. Some people branded him a snob, others a sort of metaphysical rake, but all agreed that he was an entertaining man.

He had translated the hitherto incomprehensible-seeming motto of his house, " Estre que fayre,"—"To be rather than to do." *To be :* to be on all sides a highly developed mortal,—a scholar, a connoisseur, a good talker, an amiable companion, a healthy animal,—was his aim in life, so nearly as it could be said of him that he had an aim. And therefore he played golf (it was heartrending, he declared, to see how badly), took an intelligent interest in foot-ball, read everything (save the hyperbole !) and kept abreast of what was being done in music, painting, sculpture, and keramics : in short, went heavily in for all forms of unremunerative culture. The theatre he avoided, because he deemed acting at its best but a bad reflection of the creative arts, and at its worst, as he maintained we got it nowadays, a mere infectious disease of the nervous system. Neither would he hunt, shoot, fish, nor eat of any flesh, because, he explained, it would be unpleasant to have to consider himself a beast of prey. He had a skillful cook, however, and fared sumptuously every day on such comestibles as plovers' eggs and truffles, milk, honey, fruits, and flowers (is not the laborious artichoke a flower ?), and simple bread and cheese served in half a hundred delectable disguises. He dined out, to be sure, six or seven evenings in the week; but these were Barmecide feasts for him, and on coming home he could sup. When he went to stay in the country he took his cook with him, instead of his man ; and people bore with his

eccentricities because he could say diverting things.

He was an epicure, though a vegetarian,
a cynic in a benignant, trifling way, and a
pessimist, though a debonair one.

"A little cheerful pessimism, is a great
help here below," he used to urge. "It
takes one over many a rough place. Has
it ever struck you to reflect how much
worse the world might be, if it weren't so
bad?"

Occasionally, no doubt, his pessimism
glowed with a less merry hue : when, for instance, he would be short of funds and hard
pressed by duns. "How many noble fel-
lows have fought loyally in the battle to
lead a life of sweet idleness, and fallen over-
powered by the cruel greed of tradesmen !
Am I to be of their number?" he would
ask himself sadly at such moments.

He was the most indefatigable of human
men when engaged in pursuits that were entirely profitless, like arranging picnics, go-

ing to parties, inventing paradoxes, or drinking tea ; but when it came to anything re-
motely approaching the sphere of Ought, he
was the most indolent, the most prone to pro-
crastination. Far, far too indolent, for example, to be a possible correspondent,—unless he were addressing a money-lender or a
woman,—whence it resulted that he and his
son had written to each other but desul-
torily and briefly, and knew appallingly little of each other's state of mind. Three or
four years ago the boy, having taken his
degree at Harvard, had poised for an instant
on the brink of a resolution to run over and
pay his sire a visit ; but then he had decided
to wait about doing that till he should have
put in " the requisite number of terms at
the Law School to secure his admission to
the Bar," as he expressed it.

Now, it appeared, the requisite number
had been achieved, for early in May, along
with the first whiffs of warm air, shimmers of
sunshine, and rumblings of carriage-wheels

in the Park, the elder man received a letter that ran like this :—

"My dear Father,

"You will, I am sure, be glad to know that I have passed my final examinations, and shall shortly have the right to sign LL. B. after my name, as well as to practise in the courts.

"I mean to sail for Europe on the 1st of June, by the *Teutonic*, and shall reach London about the 8th. I should like to spend the summer with you in England, familiarising myself with British institutions, and in the fall go through France and Germany, and down into Italy to pass the winter. But of course I should submit my plans to your revision.

"My grandfather and grandmother are keeping very well, and join me in love to you.

"Your affectionate son,

"Harold Weir."

"The lad seems to have some humour," was the senior Weir's reflection upon this epistle. "'British institutions' is rather droll. And if his style seems a trifle stiff in the joints, that only results from youth and a legal education. I trust to Providence, though, that he mayn't have LL.B. engraved upon his card; —these Americans are capable of anything. However I shall be glad to see him."

And he began to picture pleasantly to himself the fun that awaited him in having a well set-up young man of five and twenty, whose pockets were full of money (the maternal grandfather saw to that, thank goodness), to knock about with; and he looked forward almost eagerly to the 8th of June. They would finish the season in town together, and afterwards do a round of country houses, and then make for the Continent: and, taking one consideration with another, it would be a tremendous lark. That Harold was well set-up he knew from a photograph. His only fear on the score of ap-

pearance concerned his colouring. That
might be trying. However, he would hope
not ; and anyhow, in this world we must
take the bitter with the sweet.

He went to Euston (having had due tele-
graphic warning from Liverpool) to welcome the youth on the platform ; and he
didn't quite know whether to be pleased or
dismayed when he saw him step from a third-
class compartment of the train. It was rather smart than otherwise to travel third-class,
of course ; but how could a young American,
fresh from democracy, be aware of this somewhat recondite canon of aristocratic manners? and might the circumstance not argue,
therefore, parsimony or a vulgar taste ?

He had no doubt at all, however, about
the nature of the emotion that Harold's
hat aroused in him ; for not only was it a
"topper," but—as if travelling from Liverpool in a topper weren't in itself enough—it
had to be a topper of an outlandish, un-

English model ; and he shuddered to speculate for what plebeian provincial thing people
might have been mistaking this last fruit of
his gentle family tree. He hurried the
hat's wearer out of sight, accordingly,
into his brougham, and gave the word to
drive.

"But my baggage?" cried the son.

"Oh, my man will stop behind and look
after that. Give him your receipt."

His hat apart, Harold was really a very
presentable fellow, tall and broad-shoul-
dered, with a clear eye, a healthy brown
skin, and a generous allowance of well-
cropped brown hair ; and on the whole he
wasn't badly dressed : so that his father's
heart began to warm to him at once. His
cheeks and lips were shaven clean, like an
actor's or a priest's, whereby a certain rigidity
was imparted to the lines of his mouth. He
held himself rather rigidly too, and bolt
upright : but as his father had noticed a
somewhat similar effect in the bearing of a

good many unexceptionable young Oxford and Cambridge men, he put it down to the fashion of a generation, and didn't allow it to distress him.

"I had no idea you kept a carriage," Harold remarked, after an interval.

"Oh, I should ruin myself in cab-fares, you know," Weir explained.

"I presume London is a pretty dear city?"

"Oh, for that—shocking!" .

"I came down on the cars third-class. I want to get near the people while I am over here, and see for myself how their status compares to that of ours. I want to get a thorough idea of the economic condition of England, and see whether what David A. Wells claims for free trade is true."

"Ah, yes—yes," his father responded, dashed a little. But the boy's voice was not unpleasant ; his accent, considering whence he came, far better than could have been expected ; and as for his locutions, his choice

of words, "I must cure you of your Ameri-
canisms," the hopeful parent added.

"Sir?" the son queried, staring.

"There, to begin with, don't call me sir.
Reserve that for Royalty. I said I must try
to break you of some of your American-
isms."

"Oh, I know. The English say railway
for railroad, and box for trunk."

"Ah, if it began and ended there ! " sighed
Weir.

"But I don't see why our way isn't as
good as theirs. We've got a population of
sixty millions to their thirty, and——"

"Oh come, now ! Don't confuse the argument by introducing figures."

But at this Harold stared so hard that his
father's conscience smote him a little, and
he asked sympathetically, "I'm afraid you
take life rather seriously, don't you ? "

"Why, certainly," the young man answered with gravity. "Isn't that the way
to take it ? "

7

" Oh, bless you, no.   It's too grim a business.   The proper spirit to take it in is one of unseemly levity."

" I don't think I understand you—unless you're joking."

" You need limbering up a bit, that's all," declared his father.   " But I say, we must get you a decent hat.   Later in the day I'm going to trot you off to Mrs. Midsomer-Norton's for tea.   We'll stop at a hatter's now."   And he gave the necessary instructions to his coachman.

" What is the matter with the hat I've got on ? "

" We're not wearing that shape in London."

" What will a new one cost ? "

" Don't know, I'm sure.   Five-and-twenty shillings, I expect."

" Well, this one cost me eight dollars in Boston just about three weeks ago.   Don't you think it would be extravagant to get a new one so soon ? "

" Oh, damn the extravagance. We must 'gae fine' whatever we do."

This time there was a distinct shadow of pain in Harold's stare ; and he preserved a rueful silence till the brougham drew up at Scott's. He followed his father into the shop, however, and submitted stolidly to the operation of being fitted. When it came to paying, he pulled a very long face indeed, and appeared to have an actual mechanical difficulty in squeezing the essential coin from his purse.

"Now you look like a Christian," his father averred, as they got back into the carriage.

" I hate to throw away money, though."

" For goodness' sake don't tell me you're close-fisted."

" I don't think it's right to throw away money."

" That's a New England prejudice. You'll soon get over it here."

" I don't know. A man ought never to

be wasteful—especially with what he hasn't earned."

" Ah, there's where I can't agree with you. If a man had *earned* his money he might naturally have some affection for it, and wish to keep it. But those who like you and me are entirely vicarious in their sacrifice, and spend what other folk have done the grubbing for, can afford to be royally free-handed. "

Harold made no response, but it was evident that he had a load on his mind for the remainder of their drive.

At Mrs. Midsomer-Norton's the young man's bewilderment and melancholy seemed to deepen into something not far short of horror, as he formed one of a group about his father, and heard that personage sing-song out, with an air of intense fatigue, his flippant inconsequences.

There was a little mite of a man present, with a fat white face and a great shock of red hair, whom the others called the Bard ; and he announced that he was writing a poem in which it would be necessary to give a general definition of Woman in a single line ; and he called upon the company to help him.

" Woman," wailed Weir, languidly, as he leaned upon the mantelpiece, " Woman is —such sweet sorrow."

There was a laugh at this, in which, however, Harold could not join. Then the Bard cried, " That's too abstract ; " and Weir retorted, drawling, " Oh, if you must have her defined in terms of matter, Woman is a mass of pins." Harold slunk away into a corner, to hide his shame. He felt that his father was playing the fool outrageously.

The Bard curled himself up, cross-legged like the bearded Turk, upon the hearthrug, and repeated some verses. He called them a "villanelle," and said they were "after the French."

> " I have lost my silk umbrella,
>   Someone else no doubt has found it :
>   I would like to catch the fella !

" Or it may be a femella
      Cast her fascination round it.
   I have lost my silk umbrella.

" Male or female, beau or bella,
      Who hath ventured to impound it,
   I would like to catch the fella !

" Talk about a tourterella !
      I'd rather lose a score, confound it.
   I have lost my silk umbrella.

" It was new and it was swella !
      If I had his head I'd pound it,
   I would like to catch the fella.

" Hearken to my ritournella,
      From my heart of hearts I sound it,—
   I have lost my silk umbrella,
      I would like to catch the fella."

Everybody laughed ; but Harold thought
the verses silly and uninteresting, and full
of vain repetitions ; and he wondered that
grown-up men and women could waste
their time upon such trivialities.

On their way home he took his father
to task. "Of course you didn't mean the

things you said in that lady's house?" he
began.

"Why? Did I say anything I hadn't
oughter?"

Harold frowned in wonder at his father's
grammar, and replied severely, " You said
a good many things that you couldn't have
meant. You said a lie in time saves nine.
You said consistency is the last refuge of a
scoundrel. You said a lot of things that I
can't remember, but which seemed to me
rather queer."

"Oh, we're a dreadfully frisky set, you
know," Weir explained. Then he turned
aside for an instant, to get rid of an impor-
tunate hansom, that had sauntered after
them for a hundred yards, the driver raining
invitations upon them from his "dicky."
—"No, I *won't* be driven. I'll be led, but I
won't be driven," he said, resolutely. "You'll
get accustomed to us, though," he continued, addressing his son.

"Do you mean to say the people of your

set are always like that ?   Why, there wasn't
a single person there that you could con-
verse with seriously about anything."

"I didn't want to, I'm sure," his father
protested.

But the son's commentary was not to be
diverted.   "I asked that gentleman they
called Major what he thought the effect of
smokeless powder would be upon future
warfare ; and he looked perfectly paralysed,
and said he didn't know, he was sure.   And
that member of Parliament from Sheffingham,
I asked him what the population of Sheffingham was, and *he* didn't know.   And that
lady,—Lady Angela something,—I asked
her how she liked 'Robert Elsmere,' and
she said she didn't know him."

"I'm afraid our friends thought you had
rather a morbid appetite for information,
Harold."

"Well, I must say, I thought they were
very superficial.   All froth and glitter.
Nothing solid or genuine about them.   And

that poem that little red-haired man recited !
Now in American houses of that sort you'd
hear serious conversation."

"Your taste is austere. But you must
be charitable, you must make allowances.
Besides, some of us aren't so superficial as
you'd think. All that glitters isn't pinch-
beck. Major Northbrook, for example, is
the best polo player in England. And Lady
Angela Folbourne is very nearly the most
disreputable woman. A reg'lar bad un, you
know, and makes no bones of it, either.
Perfectly, frankly, cynically wicked. Yet
somehow or other she contrives to keep her
place in society, and goes to Court. You
see, she must have solid qualities, real abili-
ties, somewhere ? "

"How do you mean she's wicked,—in
what sense ? "

"Oh, I say ! You mustn't expect me to
dot my i's and cross my t's like that. A
sort of *société en commandite,* you know."

" You mean——? "

"Yes, quite so."

"Why, but then, gracious heavens! she's no better than a—than a professional——"

"Worse, worse, my dear. She's an amateur."

"I'm surprised you should know such a woman."

"Oh, bless you, she's a Vestal Virgin to ladies I could introduce you to across the Channel."

"How horrible!" cried the young American.

"For pity's sake, don't tell me you're a Nonconformist," his father pleaded.

"I'm an Episcopalian," the son answered. He relapsed into his stare ; and then at dinner it turned out that he was a teetotaller and didn't use tobacco.

In his diary, before he went to bed, Harold made this entry :—

"London cab-fares are sixpence a mile, with a minimum of a shilling. There are upwards of 10,000 cabs in London. The city is better paved than Boston, but not so clean. Many of the wards preserve their original parochial systems of government. The people aren't so go-ahead as ours, and the whole place lacks modernity. The tone of English society seems to be very low. To-morrow I shall visit Westminster Abbey, St. Paul's Cathedral, Hyde Park, the British Museum, and the Victoria Embankment. Qy. : what was the cost of the construction of the latter ? "

That will give a notion of the dance he led his father on the following day. Harold stared at most of the "sights," as he called them, in solemn silence. Of Westminster, however, he remarked that it was in a bad state of repair. "The English people don't seem to have much enterprise about them," he said. "Now if this were in America—" But his father did not catch the conclusion. St. Paul's struck him as surprisingly dirty. "You should see the new Auditorium in Chicago," he suggested. "I was out there last year. That's what I call fine architecture." And then, as they drove along the Embankment, he propounded his query anent its cost ; and his father cried, "If you ask me questions like that, I shall faint."

Harold's diary that night received this pathetic confidence:—

"On the whole London doesn't come up to any of the large American cities. As for my father, I hoped yesterday that he was only putting it on for a joke, but I'm afraid now that he really is very light-minded. He wears an eyeglass and speaks with a strong English accent. Expenses this day. . . " And so forth.

The elder Weir, at the same time, was likewise engaged in literary composition :—

" My Dear Mrs. Winchfied,—

"I am in great distress about my son. You don't believe I've got one ? Oh, but I give you my word ! He's just reached me from America, where I left him as a hostage

a quarter of a century ago.   And he's full of
the most awful heathenish ideas.   I never
met so serious a person.   He doesn't drink,
he doesn't smoke ; he thinks I'm undignified,
if you can imagine that ; and he objects to
my calling him Hal, though his name is
Harold.   I feel like a frisky little boy beside
him,—like the child that is father to the
man.   Then his thirst for knowledge is
positively disgraceful.   He has nearly killed
me to-day, *doing* London, guide-book in
hand, and asking *such* embarrassing questions.   Can you tell me, please, how long
the Houses of Parliament were a-build-
ing ?   And how many dollars there are in the
vaults of the Bank of England?   And what
the salary of a policeman is ?   And who is
'about the biggest lawyer over here ?'   The
way he dragged me up and down the town
was most unfilial.   We've been everywhere,
I think, except to my club.   But he's a very
good-looking fellow, and I don't doubt he's
got the right sort of stuff dormant in him

somewhere, only it wants bringing out. I
can't help feeling that what he needs is the
influence of a fine, sensitive, irresponsible
woman, someone altogether wayward and
ribald, to lighten and loosen him, and im-
part a little froth and elasticity.

"I was entirely broken-hearted when I
heard that you were going to stop at Sere all
summer ; but even for adversity there are
sweet uses ; and I wish you would ask my
boy down to stay with you. I'm sure you
can do him good, unless too many months of
country air have made a sober woman of you.
Do try to Christianise him, and a father's
heart will reward you with its blessing.

"Yours always,

"A. WEIR."

Then Harold went down to Sere ; and
a fortnight later Mrs. Winchfield wrote as
follows to his parent:—

"DEAR WEIR,—

"I'm afraid it's hopeless. I've done my

utmost, and I've failed grotesquely. Yesterday I chanced to say, in your young one's
presence, to Colonel Buttington, who's staying here, that if my husband were only
away, I should so enjoy a desperate flirtation
with him. Harold, dear boy, looked scan-
dalised, and by and by, catching me alone,
he asked (in the words of Father William's
interlocutor) whether I thought at my age it
was right? He is like the Frenchman who
took his wife to the play, and chid her when
she laughed, saying, '*Nous ne sommes pas
ici pour nous amuser.*' I am sending him
back by the morning train to morrow. Keep
him with you, and try to cultivate a few
domestic virtues. *A vous,*

" MARGARET WINCHFIELD."

Harold arrived, looking very grave. But his
father looked graver still, and he invited the
young man into the library, and gave him a
piece of his mind. It produced no sensible
effect. At last, "Well, I hope at least you

tipped the servants liberally ? " the poor man questioned.

"No, sir, I don't believe in tipping servants. What are they paid their wages for ? "

"You're quite irreclaimable," the father cried. "May I ask how long you mean to remain in England ? "

"I think I shall need about two months to do it thoroughly."

His father left the room, and gave orders to his man to pack for a long journey.

A SLEEVELESS ERRAND.

" J'ai perdu ma tourterelle,
Je veux aller après elle."

I.

It had been the old familiar story, in its most hackneyed version.

She was nineteen ; he was three or four and twenty, with an income just sufficient to keep him in bread and cheese, and for prospects and position those of an art-student in a land of money-grubbers. And her parents, who were wise in their generation, wouldn't hear of a betrothal ; whilst the young people, who were foolish in theirs, hadn't the courage of their folly. And so—the usual thing happened. They vowed eternal constancy—"If it can't be you, it sha'n't be anyone!"—and said good-bye.

He left his native hemisphere, to acquire technique in the schools of Paris; and she, after an interval of a year or two, married another man.

Yet, though in its letter their tale was commonplace enough, the spirit of it, on his side at least, was a little rare. I suppose that most young lovers love with a good deal of immediate energy; but his love proved to be of a fibre that could resist the tooth of time. At any rate, years went their way, and he never quite got over it; he was true to that conventional old vow.

This resulted in part, no doubt, from the secluded, the concentrated, manner of his life, passed aloof from actuality, in a studio *au cinquième*, alone with his colour-tubes and his ideals; but I think it was due in part also to his temperament. He was the sort of man of whom those who know him will ex-

claim, when his name comes up, "Ah yes—
the dear fellow !" Everybody liked him, and
all laughed at him more or less. He was
extremely simple-minded and trustful, very
quiet, very modest, very gentle and sym-
pathetic ; by no means without wit, nor
altogether without humour, yet in the main
disposed to take things a trifle too seriously
in a world where levity tempered by suspicion is the only safe substitute for a wholesome, whole-souled cynicism. Though an
uncompromising realist in his theories, I
suspect that down at bottom he was inclined
to be romantic, if not even sentimental. His
friends would generally change the subject
when he came into the room, because to the
ordinary flavour of men's talk he showed a
womanish repugnance. In the beginning,
on this account, they had of course voted
him a prig ; but they had ended by regarding it as a bothersome little eccentricity,
that must be borne with in view of his many
authentic virtues.

For the rest, he had a sweet voice, a good figure and carriage, a clean-cut Saxon face, and a pleasing, graceful talent, which, in the course of time, fostered by industry, had brought him an honourable mention, several medals, then the red ribbon, and at last the red rosette.

He was what they call a successful man ; and he had succeeded in a career where success carries a certain measure of celebrity : yet it was a habit of his mind to think of himself as a failure. This was partly because he had too just a real sing sense of the nature of art, to fancy that success in art— success in giving material form to the visions of the imagination—is ever possible ; an artist might be defined as one whose mission it is to fail. At all events, neither medals nor decorations could blind him to the circumstance that there was a terrible gulf between what he had intended and what he had accomplished, between the great pictures of his dreams and the canvasses that bore his signature. But in thinking of himself as a failure, I am sure he was chiefly influenced by the recollection that he had not been able to marry that dark-eyed young American girl twenty years before.

At first it had changed life to a sort of waking nightmare for him. He had come abroad with a heart that felt as if it had been crushed between the upper and the nether millstones. His ambition was dead, and his interest in the world. He could not work, because he could see no colour in the sky, and nothing but futility in art ; and he could not play,—he could not throw himself into the dissipations of the Quarter, and so benumb his hurt a little with immediate physical excitements,—because pleasure in all its forms had lost its savour. Then a kindly Providence interposed, and ordained that he should drink a glass of infected water, or breathe a mouthful of poisoned air, and fall ill of typhoid fever, and forget ; and when he was convalescent, and remembered again, he remembered this : that she had sworn on her soul to be constant to him. Whereupon he said, "I will work like twenty Trojans, and annihilate time, and earn money, and go home with an assured position ; and then her parents can have no further pretext for withholding their consent." In this resolution he found great comfort.

He had been working like twenty Trojans for about a twelvemonth, when he got the news of her marriage to the other man.

It chanced to reach him (in a letter from a friend, saying it would be celebrated in a fortnight) on the very day of its occurrence ; and that, by a pleasant co-incidence, was his birthday. In a fit of cynical despair he asked a lot of his school-fellows, and a few ladies of the neighbour-hood, to dine with him ; and they feasted and made merry till well into the following morning, when, for the first and almost the only time in his life, he had to be helped home, drunk. His drunkenness, though, was perhaps not altogether to be regretted. It kept him from thinking ; and for that particular night it was conceivably better, on the whole, that he should not think.

His mood of cynical recklessness lasted for a month or two. He celebrated the wedding—*faisait la noce*, as the local idiom runs—in a double sense, and with feverish diligence. For a moment it seemed a toss-up what would become of him : whether he would sink into the condition of a chronic *noceur*, or return to the former decent tenor of his way. It happened, however, that he had no appetite for alcohol, and that bad music, bad air, evil communications, gaslight, and late hours failed to afford him any permanent satisfaction : whilst, as for other women,—who that has savoured nectar can care for milk and water?—who that has lost a rose can be consoled with an artificial flower? This was how he put it to himself. All the women he knew on the right bank of the Seine were, to his taste, mortally insipid ; those whom he knew on the left were stuffed with sawdust.

And the consequence was that one morning he went to work again ; and in spite of the dull pain in his heart, he worked steadily, doggedly, from day to day, from year to year, scarcely noting the progress of time, in the absorbed and methodical nature of his life, till presently he had turned forty, and was what they call a successful man. Of course the dull pain in his heart had softened gradually into something that was not entirely painful ; into something whose sadness was mixed with sweetness, like plaintive music ; but her image remained enshrined as an idol in his memory, and I doubt if ever a day passed without his spending some portion thereof in worship before it. He never walked abroad, either, through the Paris streets, without thinking, "What if I should meet her !" (It would be almost inevitable that she should some time come to Paris.) And at this prospect his heart would leap and his pulses quicken like a boy's. For art and love between them had kept him young ; it had indeed never struck him to count his lustres, or to reflect that in point of them he was middle-aged. Besides, he lived in a country whose amiable custom it is to call every man a lad until he marries. Regularly once a year, in the autumn, he had sent a picture to be exhibited at New York, in the hope that she might see it.

He gave his brushes to be washed rather earlier than usual this afternoon, and went for a stroll in the garden of the Luxembourg. The air was languorous with the warmth and the scent of spring; in the sunshine the marble queens, smiling their still, stony smile, gleamed with a thousand tints of rose and amethyst, as if they had been carved of some iridescent substance, like mother-of-pearl. The face of the old palace glowed with mellow fire ; the sleek, dark-green foliage of the chestnut-trees was tipped here and there with pallid gold ; and in the deep

shade of the *allées* underneath innumerable
children romped vociferously, and innumerable pairs of lovers sentimentalised in
silence.   Of course they were only mock'
lovers, students and their *étudiantes;* but
one could forget that for the moment, and
all else that is ugly, in the circumambient
charm.

He took a penny chair by and by, and
sat down at the edge of the terrace, and
watched the dance of light and shadow on the
waters of the fountain, and thanked Heaven
for the keen, untranslatable delight he was
able to feel in the beauty of the world.   He
drank it in with every sense, as if it were
an ethereal form of wine ; but no wine was
so delicious, no wine could have penetrated
and thrilled and stimulated him as it did.   It
was a part of his philosophy,—I might almost
say an article of his religion,—to count his
faculty for deriving exquisite pleasure from
every phase of the beautiful as in some sort a
compensation for many of the good things

of life that he had missed; and yet, in one
way at least, so far from serving as a compensation, it only added to his loss. In the
presence of whatever was beautiful, under
the spell of it, he always longed with inten-
sified pain for her. And now presently, as
he had done in like circumstances countless
times before, he sighed for her, inwardly :
"Ah, if she were here ! If we could enjoy
it all together ! "—I dare say, poor man, it
was a little ridiculous at his age ; but he did
not see the humour.

He pictured her to himself, her slender
figure, her white, eager face, with its pe-
numbra of brown hair, soft as smoke, and its
dark eyes, deep and luminous, as if pale
fires were burning infinitely far within
them. He heard her voice, low and melo-
dious, and her crisp, girlish laughter. And
she smiled upon him, a faint, sad smile,
that was full of tenderness and yearning
and regret. He took her hands, her warm
little rosy hands, and marvelled over them,

as he caressed them. They were like images in miniature of herself, so sensitive, so fragile, so helpless-seeming, yet possessed of such amazing talents : for when he watched them leaping above the ivory keys of her piano, invariably striking the right note with the right degree of stress and the right interval of time (although to an uninitiated witness their movement must have appeared quite wanton), he wondered at them as a pair of witches.

If he had not reckoned his own years, or marked their action upon himself, it is certain that he had treated her with no less forbearance. She came back to him always the same ; always the girl of nineteen whom he had left behind him nearly a quarter of a century ago.

Ah, if she were only with him now, here in the quaint old garden of the Luxembourg ! How complete and unutterable his joy would be ! He would lead her beside the great basin of the fountain, where the goldfishes flashed like flames ; and they would stop before the statues of the queens, and tell over for each other the romantic histories of those dead royal ladies ; and how much warmer the sunshine would be, how much greener the earth, how much sweeter the fragrance of the air ! By and by they would enter the museum, where he would show her that picture of his which the State had honoured him by buying, and which, he had received a whispered promise, should some day find its way into the Louvre. Afterwards they would saunter down the Boulevard, past the Castle of Cluny, across the bridge, into the open space before Notre Dame. And all the while they would talk, talk, talk, making up for the time that they had lost ; and their wounds would be healed, and their hearts would be at rest. It was strange, he thought, that she had never come abroad. All Americans come sooner or later, and one is perpetually running across those one happens to know.

He had never run across her, however, though he had never left off expecting to do so. This very afternoon, for instance, how entirely natural it would seem to meet her. The annual irruption of his country-people had begun; thousands of them were in Paris at this moment : why not she among them ? And she would certainly not come to Paris without visiting the Luxembourg ; and to-day was a perfect day for such a visit ; and—if he should look up now . . . .

He looked up, holding his breath for a second, almost thinking to see her advancing towards him. Surely enough, somebody *was* advancing towards him, standing before him there in the path, making signals to him. But, as the mists of his day-dream cleared away, he perceived that it was only the old woman come to take his penny for the chair.

He went home, a very lonely man in a very empty world.

It felt cold to him now; the sky had

grown gray. He had a fire kindled in his drawing-room, and sat dejectedly before it through the twilight. After a while his servant brought in the lamps, at the same time handing him a parcel that had come from his bookseller's. The parcel was wrapped in an old copy of the Paris edition of the *New York Herald;* and he spread it out, and glanced at it listlessly. It always filled him with a vague sort of melancholy to look at an old newspaper; on the day of its appearance the life that it recorded, the joys and pains, had seemed of so great importance, such instant interest ; and now they mattered as little, they were as much a part of ancient history, as the lives and the joys and the sorrows of the Cæsars. His eye fell presently upon a column headed *Obituary*; and there he read of the death of Samuel Merrow. He turned the paper up hurriedly to discover its date; November of last year; quite six months ago. Samuel Merrow had died at New York, six months ago ; and Samuel Merrow was her husband.

II

THERE were not many passengers on the steamer; at this season the current of travel ran in the opposite direction. There was a puffy little white-haired, important man, who accosted him on the deck, the second day out, and asked whether it was his first visit abroad that he was returning from. He reflected for a moment, and answered yes; for though he had lived abroad half a lifetime, he had crossed the ocean only once before. He was too shy to enter upon an explanation, so he answered yes. Then the puffy man boasted of the immense numbers of voyages *he* had made. "Oh, I know Europe!" he declaimed, and told how his business—he described himself as "buyer" for a firm of printing-ink importers

—took him to that continent two or three times a year. He had an inquiring mind, and a great facility for questioning people. "Excuse me, Mr. Aigrefield," he said (he had learned our friend's name from the passenger-list) "but what does that red button in your buttonhole mean? Some society you belong to?"

Aigrefield, concealing what he suffered, again sought refuge in an ambiguous yes; but he slunk away to his cabin, and put the "red button" in his box: it was absurd to wear the insignia of a French order outside of France.

Then, of course, the ship's company was completed by a highly intelligent lady in eyeglasses, who lay in a deck-chair all day, and read Mr. Pater's *Marius* (the volume lasted her throughout the voyage); a statistical clergyman, returning from his vacation, a mine of practical misinformation; a couple of Frenchmen, travelling no one could guess why, since they seemed quite cast-down

9

and in despair about it ; a half-dozen He-
brews, travelling one couldn't help knowing wherefore, since they discussed "vool-
lens" and prices and shipments at the tops
of their cheerful voices ; and the inevitable
young Western girl, travelling alone. For
the first time in twenty years, almost, he
had descended from the cloud he lived in,
and was rubbing against the actualities of
the earth.

The highly intelligent lady "knew who he
was," as she told him sweetly, and would
speak of nothing but art, in her highly intelligent way. If he had had more humour,
her perfervid enthusiasms, couched in an extremely rudimental studio-slang (she talked
a vast deal of values and keys, of atmosphere
and light, of things being badly modelled or
a little "out")—if he had had more humour,
all this might have amused him ; but he
was, as we have said, somewhat too literally
inclined ; and the cant of it jarred upon him,
and made him sick at heart. Her formula

for opening up a topic, "Now, Mr. Aigrefield, tell me, what do you think of . . . "
became an obsession, that would descend
upon him in the dead of night, making him
dread the morrow.

All these people, he remarked, Mr. Aigre-
fielded him unpityingly. He wished the
English language had, for the use of his
compatriots (in England they seem to get
on well enough without forever naming
names) a mode of address similar to the
French *monsieur*.

But the solitary young Western girl he
liked. She had made her first appeal to his
eye, through her form and colour; but when
he came to know her a little he liked her
for her spirit. She was tall, with a strong,
supple figure, a face picturesque in the discreet irregularity of its features, a pair of
limpid gray eyes, a fresh complexion, and
an overhanging ornament of warm brown
hair. She was much given to smiling, also,
—a smile that played in lovely curves about

lips, if anything, a thought too full, a semi-
tone too scarlet,—whence he inferred that
she had an amiable disposition, a light
heart, and an easy conscience. Hearing
her speak, he observed that her voice was
of a depth, smoothness, and rotundity, that
atoned in great measure for the occidental
quality of her accent. At all events, he was
drawn to her : they walked the deck a good
deal together, and often had their chairs
placed side by side. He philosophised her
attraction for him by saying, "She is a force
of nature, she is fresh and simple." The
"buyer" for the firm of printing-ink importers had struck him as fresh, indeed, but
not as simple ; the lady who read Mr. Pater,
as simple but not fresh ; the Hebrew gentle-
men, even the unhappy Frenchmen, if you
will, as natural forces : but the Western girl
combined these several advantages in her
single person, and so she became his
favourite amongst his shipmates.

Her name was Lillian Goddard ; she lived

in Minneapolis, where, as she informed him, her father was a judge. She had been abroad nearly a year, had passed the winter in Rome, could speak a little Italian, a little French, and an immense deal of American. I have described her as young, and I hope it will not be considered an anachronism when I add that her age was twenty-six.

She was tremendously patriotic, and appeared shocked and grieved when she learned that he had remained continuously absent from his country for a score of years.

"Why, the more I saw of Europe, the more I loved dear old America," she declared, in her deep voice.

She was just as homesick as she could be, she said, and couldn't get back to Minneapolis fast enough. Did he know the West? —and again she appeared shocked at discovering the profundities of his ignorance concerning it. Oh, he must certainly see the West. No American could begin to appreciate his country till he had seen the

West. The people out there were so *alive*,
so go-ahead ; and they took such an interest
in all forms of culture too, in literature,
music, painting, the drama. "Why, look
at the big magazines,—they depend for their
circulation on the West." And then, the
homes of the West! "Oh, if I lived in
Europe, I should lose my faith in human
nature. Western people are so warm-
hearted. I'm afraid you're awfully un-
patriotic, Mr. Aigrefield."

He reminded her that patriotism was the
last refuge of a scoundrel ; and anyhow, he
pleaded, it was too much to expect of one
small man that he should be patriotic for
a continent. But she shook her head at
his perversity, and guessed he'd be proud
enough of his Continent if he had seen it,
and insisted that he must come to Minneapolis, and look round.

He liked her amazingly. As their voyage
grew older, he found himself taking a
greater and greater pleasure in her pro-

pinquity ; looking forward with something
akin to eagerness to meeting her on deck,
as he accomplished his morning toilet ; and
recalling fondly their commerce of the day,
as he turned in at night. Besides, the charm
of her strong, irregular beauty grew upon
him, and he said to her, smiling, "When I
come to Minneapolis you must let me try a
portrait of you."

"Ah, then you are really coming?" she
demanded, striving to fix him in a pious
resolution.

He laughed vaguely, and she protested,
" Oh, shame, Mr. Aigrefield, now you are
wriggling out ! "

He felt that she was sweet and sound and
honest : direct, vigorous, bracing : he wondered if indeed she might not owe these
qualities, in some part, to her native Western
soil ; and he admitted that the West was beginning to take a place in his affections.
Heretofore, it had been a mere geographical
abstraction for him, and one he would have

shrunk from realising through experience. He imagined the colouring would be hard, the action violent, the atmosphere raw and rough.

"Well, whether I really come or not, I am sure I should really like to," he said now.

"That's such an innocent desire," she cried, with a touch of mockery. "I don't think it would be selfish to indulge it."

"And if I do come, you will sit for me?"

"Oh, I'd do anything in such a cause— to make a patriot of you!"

At the outset of his journey, his impatience to reach the end of it was so great, the progress of the steamer had seemed exasperatingly slow. But as they began to near New York, a vague dread of what might await him there, a vague recoil from the potential and the unknown, made him almost wish that the throbbing of the engines were not so rapid. A cloud of dismal possibilities haunted his imagination, filling it with a strange chill and ache. He had never paused

before to think of the many things that
had had time to happen in twenty years ;
and now they assailed his mind in a mass,
and appalled it. Even the preliminary
business of discovering her whereabouts, for
instance, might prove difficult enough ; and
then——? In matters of this sort, at any
rate, it is the next step which costs. In
twenty years what ties and affections she
might have formed, that would make him a
necessary stranger to her life, and leave no
room for him in her heart. He was jealous
of a supposititious lover (he had lived in
France too long to remember that in America lovers are not the fashion), of supposititious children, supposititious interests and
occupations : jealous and afraid. And of
course it was always to be reckoned with
as in the bounds of the conceivable, that she
might be disconsolate for the loss of Mr.
Merrow : though this, for some reason,
seemed the least likely of the contingencies
he had to face. Mr. Merrow, he knew, had

been a cotton-broker ; he had always fancied him as a big, rather florid person, with a husky voice : capable perhaps of inspiring a mild fondness, but not of a character to take hold upon the deeper emotional strands of Pauline's nature.

His nervousness increased inordinately after the pilot came aboard. He marched rapidly backwards and forwards on the deck, scarcely conscious of what he was saying to Miss Goddard, who kept pace with him. She laughed presently—her deep contralto laughter ; and then he inquired very seriously whether he had said anything absurd.

"Don't you *know* what you said ? " she exclaimed.

"I—I don't just remember. I was thinking of something else," he confessed, knitting his brows.

"Well, that's not very complimentary to me, now, is it ? Still, if you can say such things without knowing it, I suppose I must forgive you. I asked you what you thought was the best short definition of life, and you said a chance to make mistakes."

"I never could have said anything so good if I had had my wits about me," he explained.

Countless old memories and associations were surging up within him now ; and as he leaned over the rail and gazed into the murky waters of the New York Bay, the European chapters of his life became a mere parenthesis, and the text joined itself to the word at which it had been interrupted when he was four and twenty. Sorry patriot though he might be, he was still made of flesh and blood ; and he could not approach the land of his childhood, his youth, his love and loss, without some stirrings of the heart-strings besides those that were evoked by the prospect of meeting her. His other old companions would no doubt be dead or scattered ; or they would have forgotten him as he, indeed, till yesterday had forgotten them. Anyhow, he would not attempt to look them up. He knew that he should feel an alien among his own people ; he would not heighten the dreariness of that situation by ferreting out former intimates to find himself unrecognized, or by inquiring about them to be told that they were dead. He hadn't very clearly formulated his positive intentions, but they probably lay in his sub-consciousness, brief and to the point, if somewhat short-sighted and unpractical : he would do his wooing as speedily as might be, and bear his bride triumphantly over-sea, to his home in Paris.

He bade Miss Goddard good-bye on the dock, whilst his trunks were being rifled by the Custom House inspector.

"Now, mind, you are to come to Minneapolis," she insisted, as her hand lay in his, returning its pressure ; and he could perceive a shade of earnestness behind the smile that lighted up her eyes.

"Good-bye, good-bye," he answered, fervently, moved all at once by a feeling he would have had some difficulty in naming. "I may surprise you by turning up there one of these days."

Then her hand was withdrawn, and she disappeared in a hackney-carriage. He went back to the task of getting his luggage examined, with a sense of having been abandoned by his last friend.

"What fortitude it must require to live here," was the reflection that made him shake his head, as he drove over the rough paving-stones, through the dirty, ignoble streets, to his hotel. It struck him as more depressing still, when he emerged from the sordid tangle of the lower town into the smug rectangularity of the upper. He was sure that Pauline would be glad enough to exchange it all for the airy perspectives, the cleanliness, the gay colours, the variety of Paris. Of course he would have to give up his bachelor chambers overlooking the Luxembourg. He would rent, or buy, or even build, a proper house for her, in the

quarter of the Etoile, or near the Parc Monceau.

He turned over the pages of the Directory
that the hotel-clerk condescendingly pointed
out to him, and found that Mr. Merrow's
address had been twenty-something in a
street that had no name, but only a number
and a point of the compass to serve for one ;
and that seemed to him in thorough keeping
with the unimaginative, business-like character of the deceased cotton-broker. Pauline,
in her widowhood, would very likely have
moved away.   It was too late to make a call
to-day, being nearly dinner-time (he had
forgotten that in New York it is not forbidden
to call after dinner), but he would write her a
little note, informing her of his arrival, and
proposing to come to-morrow in the forenoon.
On the corner of the envelope he would put
"Please forward," to anticipate the event of
her having moved.   Then he could leave it
to destiny and the post-office authorities to
do the rest.

III

THE Fifth Avenue reached out in an end-less straight line before him, the prose of its architecture being obscured by the gathering twilight, and punctuated monotonously by the street-lamps. Attached to one of these he found a letter-box presently, and into it he dropped the note that he had written. '' Does Mrs. Merrow—Pauline Lake that was —remember Henry Aigrefield? And if so, may he call upon her to-morrow at eleven ? " That was how, after destroying a dozen sheets of paper, he had at last contrived to phrase his message.

He walked slowly up the long Avenue, cut at right angles, and at fixed intervals of two hundred feet, by streets that looked enough like one another to suggest the notion that they had all been cast in the

same dreary mould, and furnished to the
municipality ready-made ; past the innumerable coffee-coloured houses, with their dam-
nable iteration of rigid little doorsteps ; and
he wondered at the purblind complacency
of a people who could honestly regard this as
among the finest thoroughfares of the world.
The region he was traversing reminded him
of certain melancholy acres in the south of
London, where the city-clerk has his humble,
cheerless home : it was such a neighbourhood
grown rich and pretentious, but in nowise
mellowed or beautified.

Would *she* live in one of these insignifi-
cant boxes of brown stone? " 26, E. 51," the
address he had read in the Directory, sounded sufficiently unpromising. It had been
Mr. Merrow's house, and Mr. Merrow had
been a practical New Yorker. But the interior? He pictured the interior as entirely
lovely and delightful, for, in the nature of
things, the interior would owe its character
to Mr. Merrow's wife. A good distemper

on the walls, something light in key, yet
warm—brick-dust, or a pearly, rosy gray ;
simple, graceful chairs and tables ; a few
good pictures, numberless good books in
good bindings : over all the soft glow of candlelight ; and in the midst of all, giving unity
and meaning to it all, a lady, a tall slender
lady, in a black gown, with a pale serious
face, dark eyes full of sleeping fire, and above
her white brow a rich shadow of brown hair.
She was reading, her head bent a little, her
feet resting on a small tabouret of some dull
red stuff that lent depth to the bottom of
the picture, while the candlelight playing
upon her hair, upon her cheek and throat,
upon the ivory page of her book and the
hand that held it, made the upper and middle portions radiant. After twenty years
how little changed she was ! Her face
had lost nothing of its girlish delicacy, its
maiden innocence, it had only gained a quality of firmness, of seriousness and strength.
He found a woman where he had left a

10

child, but the woman was only the child ripened and ennobled. As the door opened to admit him, she raised her eyes, puzzled for a moment, not seeing who he was ; but then, suddenly, she stood up and moved towards him, calling his name, very low, very low, so that it fell upon his ears like a note of music. And his heart pounded suffocatingly, and he trembled deliciously in all his limbs.

Why, he began to ask himself now, why, after all, should he put off till to-morrow the realisation of this great joy ? If it was unconventional to pay a call in the evening, she, who had never been a stickler for the conventionalities, would forgive it to the ardour and the impatience of his passion. He had waited for her twenty years ; that was long enough, without adding to it another interminable period of twelve hours. Anyhow, there could be no harm in his ringing the bell of No. 26, E. 51, and inquiring whether she still lived there, and, if not, whither she had gone. Thereby a further saving of precious hours might be effected ; and—and he would do it.

The house, indeed, appeared in no particular different to the multitude that he had left behind him ; but he could have embraced the Irish maid-servant who opened the door for him, because to both of his questions she answered yes. Yes, Mrs. Merrow lived here ; and yes, she was at home. Would he walk into the parlour, please, and what name should she say? Lest the name should get perverted in its transmission, he equipped her with his card. Then he sat down in the "parlour" to await his fate.

It was a bare room, and, by the glare of the gas that lighted it, he saw that the influence of Mr. Merrow had penetrated at least thus far beyond his threshold. The floor was covered by a carpet in the flowery taste of 1860. The chairs were upholstered in thick, hot-hued plush, with a geometric pattern embossed upon it. A vast procession of little vases and things in porcelain, multiplied by the mantel-mirror and the pier-glass, shed an added forlornness on the spaces they were meant to decorate, but only cluttered up. Pauline's domain, he concluded, would be above stairs.

The door swung open after a few minutes, and he rose, with a sudden heart-leap, to greet her. But no—it was only a fat, uninteresting-looking woman (a visitor, a sister-in-law, he reasoned swiftly) come to make Pauline's excuses, probably, if she kept him waiting. He noticed that the fat lady was in mourning; and that confirmed his guess that she would prove to be a relative of the late Mr. Merrow. She wore her hair in a series of stiff ringlets ("bandelettes" I believe they are technically called) over a high, sloping forehead; the hair was thin and stringy, so that, he told himself, her brother had no doubt been bald. Two untransparent eyes gazed placidly out of the white expanses of

her face ; and he thought, as he took her in,
that she might serve as an incarnation of all
the dulness and platitude that he had felt in
the air about him from the hour of his landing in New York.

However, he stood there, silent, making
a sort of interrogative bow, and waiting for
her to state her business.

She had seemed to be studying him with
some curiosity, of a mild, phlegmatic kind,
from which he argued that perhaps she was
not wholly unenlightened about his former
relation to her brother's widow.   But now
he experienced a distinct spasm of horror,
as she threw her head to one side, and,
opening her lips, remarked lymphatically,
in a resigned, unresonant voice, " Well, I
declare !   Is that you, Harry Aigrefield?
Why, you're as gray as a rat ! "

He sank back into his chair, overwhelmed
by the abrupt disenchantment ; and he understood that it was reciprocal.

IV

He sat, inert, amid the pieces of his broken idol, for perhaps a half hour, and chatted with Mrs. Merrow of various things. She asked him if he was still as crazy about painting pictures as he used to be : to which he answered, with a hollow laugh, that he feared he was. Well, she said, playfully, she presumed there always had to be some harum-scarum people in the world; and added that "Sam" had "simply coined money" as a cotton-broker, and left her very well off. He had died of pneumonia, following an attack of the "grip."

"I suppose it seems kind of funny to you, getting back to America after so many years?" she queried, languidly. "Things are considerably changed."

He admitted that this was true, and bade

her good-night. She went with him to the door, where she gave him an inelastic handshake, accompanied by an invitation to call again.

In his bedroom at the hotel he sat before his window till late into the night, smoking cigarettes, and trying to pull himself together. The last lingering afterglow of his youth had been put out ; and therewith the whole colour of the universe was altered. He felt that he had reversed the case of the *bourgeois gentilhomme*, and been dealing in bad poetry for twenty years,—in other words, making a sentimental ass of himself; and his chagrin at this was as sharp as his grief over his recent disillusion.

Samuel Merrow was dead, but so was Pauline Lake ; or perhaps Pauline Lake, as he had loved her, had never existed outside of his own imagination. At any rate, Henry Aigrefield was dead, dead as the leaves of last autumn ; and this was another man, who wore his clothes and bore his name.

He glanced at his looking-glass, and he saw indeed, as he had lately been reminded, that this new, respectable-appearing, middle-aged personage was "as gray as a rat,"— though he did not like the figure better for its truth. It required several hours of hard mental labour to get the necessary readjustment of his faculties so much as started. The past had ceased to be the most important fraction of time for him ; the present and the future had become of moment.

In the dust and confusion of his wreck, only one thing was entirely clear : he couldn't stand New York. But the question where to go was as large as the circumference of the earth. Straight back to Paris ? Or what of that other region he had heard so much about during the past few days, the West ? By and by the form of Miss Lillian Goddard began to move refreshingly in and out among his musings ; he pictured the smile with which she would welcome him, if, by chance, he should turn his steps towards Minneapolis. It was a smile that seemed to promise a hundred undefined pleasantnesses, and it warmed his heart. "If I should go to Minneapolis——" he began; then he sat stockstill in his chair for twenty minutes; and then he got up with the air of a man who has taken a vigorous resolve.

As he undressed, he hummed softly to himself a line or two of his favourite poet,—

> " That shall be to-morrow,
> Not to-night:
> I must bury sorrow
> Out of sight."

A LIGHT SOVEREIGN.

I.

. . . . The cause of the uproar proved to
be simple enough.

Emerging into the Bischofsplatz, from the
street that I had followed, I found a great
crowd gathered before the Marmorhof, shout-
ing, "Death to Conrad!" and "Where is
Mathilde?" with all the force of its collective
lungs. The Marmorhof was the residence
of Prince Conrad, brother to the reigning
Grand Duke Otto—reigning, indeed, but now
very old and ill, and like to die. The legit-
imate successor to the throne would have
been Otto's grand-daughter, Mathilde, the
only surviving child of his eldest son, Franz-

Victor, who had been dead these ten years. But the Grand Duke's brother, Conrad, was covetous of her rights ; covetous, and, as her friends alleged, unscrupulous. For a long while, it was said, Mathilde had been in terror of her life. Conrad was unscrupulous, and, were she but out of the way, Conrad would come to reign. Rumour, indeed, whispered that he had made three actual attempts to compass her death : two by poison, one by the dagger, each, thanks to some miracle, unsuccessful. But, a fortnight since, upon the first supervention of fatal symptoms in the malady of poor old Otto, Mathilde had mysteriously disappeared. Her whereabouts unknown, all X—— was in commotion.

"She has fled and is in hiding," surmised some people, "to escape the designs of her wicked uncle." "No," retorted others, "but he, the wicked uncle himself, has kidnapped and sequestered her, perhaps even made away with her. Who can tell?"

As an inquiring stranger, the situation
interested me, and, from the top of a con-
venient doorstep, I gazed now upon this
deep-voiced Teutonic mob with a good
deal of curiosity.

It must have numbered upwards of a
thousand individuals, compact in its centre
and near the palace, but scattering towards
its edges ; a sea of faces, of pale, frowning
faces ; a surging, troubled sea. Young
men's faces for the most part ; many of
them beardless. "Students from the University," I guessed.

My own station was at the outskirts of
the assemblage, the station of a casual
spectator. Sharing my door-step with me
were a couple of sharp-faced priests, two or
three prettyish young girls—bareheaded,
presumably escaped from some of the neigh-
bouring shops—and a young man with a
pointed black beard, rather long black hair,
and a broad-brimmed, soft felt hat, who
somehow looked as if he might be a member

of that guild to which I myself belonged, the ancient and questionable company of artists.

To him I addressed myself for information.... "Students, I suppose?"

"Yes, their leaders are students. The students and the artisans of the town are of the princess's party. The army, the clergy, and the country folk are for the prince." He had discerned from my accent that I was a foreigner: whence, doubtless, the fulness of his answer.

"It seems a harmless mob enough," I suggested. "They make a lot of noise, to be sure; but that breaks no bones."

"There's just the point," said he. "The princess's friends fight only with their throats. Otherwise the present complication might never have arisen."

Meanwhile the multitude continued to shout its loudest; and for Conrad, on the whole, the quarter-hour must have been a bad one.

Presently, however, the call of a bugle wound in the distance, and drew nearer and nearer, till the bugler in person appeared, gorgeous in uniform, mounted upon a white horse, advancing slowly up the Bischofsplatz, towards the crowd, trumpeting with all his might.

" What is the meaning of that?" I asked.

" A signal to disperse," answered my companion. "He looks like a major-general, doesn't he? But he's only a trumpet-sergeant, and he's followed at a hundred yards by a battalion of infantry. His trumpet-blast is by way of warning. Disperse! Or, if you tarry, beware the soldiery!"

"His warning does not seem to pass unheeded," I remarked.

"Oh, they're a chicken-hearted lot, these friends of the princess," he assented contemptuously.

Already the mob had begun to melt. In a few minutes only a few stragglers in knots here and there were left, amongst them my acquaintance and myself.

He was a handsome young fellow, with a thin dark face, bright brown eyes, and a voice so soft that if I had heard without seeing him, I should almost have supposed the speaker to be a woman.

"We, too, had better be off," said he.

"And prove ourselves also chicken-hearted?" queried I.

"Oh, discretion is the better part of valour," he returned.

"But I should like to see the arrival of the military," I submitted.

"Ha! Like or not, I'm afraid you'll have to now," he cried. "Here they come."

With a murmurous tramp, tramp, they were pouring into the Bischofsplatz from the side streets leading to it.

"We must take to our heels," said my young man.

"We were merely on-lookers," said I.

"Conscious innocence," laughed he. "Nevertheless, we had better run for it."

And, with our fellow loiterers, we began ignominiously to run away. But before we had run far we were stopped by the voice of an officer.

"Halt! Halt! Halt, or we fire!"

As one man we halted. The officer rode up to us, and, with true military taciturnity, vouchsafed not a word either in question or explanation, but formed us in ranks of four abreast, and surrounded us with his men. Then he gave the command to march. We were, perhaps, two dozen captives, all told, and a good quarter of our number were women.

"What are we in for now?" I wondered aloud.

"Disgrace, decapitation, deprivation of civil rights, or, say, a night in the Castle of St. Michael, at the very least," replied my friend, shrugging his shoulders.

"Ah, that will be romantic," said I, feeling like one launched upon a life of adventure.

II

HE was right. We were marched across the town and into the courtyard of the Castle of St. Michael. By the time we got there, and the heavy oaken gates were shut behind us, it was nearly dark.

"Here you pass the night," announced our officer. "In the morning—humph, we will see."

"Do you mean to say they are going to afford us no better accommodation than this?" I demanded.

"So it seems," replied the dark young man. "Fortunately, however, the night is warm, the skies are clear, and to commune with the stars is reputed to be elevating for the spirit."

Our officer had vanished into the castle, leaving us a corporal and three privates as a guard of honour. We, the prisoners, gathered together in the middle of the court-yard, and held a sort of impromptu indignation meeting. The women were especially eloquent in their complaints. Two of these I recognized as having been among my neighbours of the door-step, and we exchanged compassionate glances. The other four were oldish women. who wore caps and aprons, and looked like servants.

"Cooks," whispered my comrade. "Some good burghers will be kept waiting for their suppers. Oh, what a lark!"

Our convention finally broke up with a resolution to the effect that, though we had been most shabbily treated, there was nothing to be done.

" We must suffer and be still. Let us make ourselves as comfortable as we can, and seek distraction in an interchange of ideas," proposed my mate. He seated himself upon a barrel that lay lengthwise against the castle wall, and motioned to me to place myself beside him.

"You are English?" he inquired, in an abrupt German way.

"No, I am American."

"Ah, it is the same thing. A tourist?"

"You think it is the same thing?" I questioned sadly. "You little know. But—— yes, I am a tourist."

"Have you been long in X——?"

"Three days."

"For heaven's sake, what have you found to keep you here three days?"

"I am a painter. The town is paintable."

"Still life! *Nature morte!*" he cried. "It is the dullest little town in Christendom. But I'm glad you are a painter. I am a musician—a fiddler."

"I suspected we were of the same ilk," said I.

"Did you, though? That was shrewd. But I, too, seemed to scent a kindred soul."

"Here is my card. If we're not beheaded in the morning, I hope we may see more of each other," I went on, warming up.

He took my card, and, by the light of a match struck for the occasion, read aloud, "Mr. Arthur Wainwright," pronouncing the English name without difficulty. "I have no card, but my name is Sebastian Roch."

"You speak English?" was my inference.

"Oh, yes, I speak a kind of English," he confessed, using the tongue in question. He had scarcely a trace of a foreign accent.

"You speak it uncommonly well."

"Oh, I learned it as a child, and then I have relatives in England."

"Do you suppose there would be any objection to our smoking?" I asked.

"Oh, no! let us smoke by all means."

I offered him my cigarette case. Our cigarettes afire, we resumed our talk.

"Tell me, what in your opinion is the truth about Mathilde?" I began. "Is she in voluntary hiding, or is her uncle at the bottom of it?"

"Ah, that is too hard a riddle," he protested. "I know nothing about it, and I have scarcely an opinion. But I may say very frankly that I am not of her partisans. She has no worse enemy than I."

"What! Really? I'm surprised at that. I thought all the youth of X—— were devoted to her."

"She's a harmless enough person in her way, perhaps, and I have nothing positive to charge against her; only I don't think she's made of the stuff for a reigning monarch. She's too giddy, too light-headed; she thinks too little of her dignity. Court ceremonial is infinitely tiresome to her; and the slow, dead life of X—— she fairly hates. Harmless, necessary X—— she has been known to call it. She was never meant to be the captain of this tiny ship of State; and with such a crew! You should see the ministers and courtiers! Dry

bones and parchment, puffed up with
tedious German eddigette! She was born
a Bohemian, an artist, like you or me.
I pity her, poor thing—I pity everyone
whose destiny it is to inhabit this dreary
Principality—but I can't approve of her.
She, too, by-the-by, plays the violin. My
own thought is, beware of fiddling mon-
archs!"

"You hint a Nero."

"Say a Nero crossed with a Haroun-al-
Raschid. I fear her reign would be diversi-
fied by many a midnight escapade, like
the merry Caliph's, only without his inter-
mixture of wrong-righting. She'd seek her
own amusement solely ; though to seek that
in X—— ! you might as well seek for blood
in a broomstick. Oh, she'd make no end of
mischief. The devil hath no agent like a
woman bored."

"That's rather true." I agreed, laughing.
"And Conrad? What of him?"

"Oh, Conrad's a beast ; a squint-eyed,

calculating beast. But a beast might make a good enough Grand Duke ; and anyhow, a beast is all that a beastly little Grand Duchy like this deserves. However, to tell you my secret feeling, I don't believe he'll have the chance to prove it. Mathilde, for all her ennui, is described as tenacious of her rights, and as a cleverish little body, too, down at bottom.. That is inconsistent, but there's the woman of it. I can't help suspecting, somehow, that unless he has really killed and buried her, she will contrive by hook or crook to come to her throne."

That night was long, though we accomplished a lot of talking : cold it seemed, too, though we were in midsummer. I dozed a little, with the stone wall of the castle for my pillow, half-conscious all the while that Sebastian Roch was carrying on a bantering flirtation with the two young girls. At daybreak our guard was changed. At six o'clock we were visited by a dapper little lieutenant, who looked us over, asked our names and other personal questions, scratched his chin for a moment reflectively, and finally, with an air of inspiration, bade us begone. The gates were thrown open and we issued from our prison, free.

" It's been almost a sensation," said Sebastian Roch. "So one can experience almost a sensation, even in X—— ! Live and learn."

" You are not a patriot," said I.

" My dear sir, I am patriotism incarnate. Only I find my country dull. If that be treason, make the most of it. I could not love thee, dear, so well, loved I not dulness less. It is not every night of my life that I am arrested, and sit on a barrel smoking cigarettes with an enlightened foreigner. The English are not generally accounted a lively race, but by comparison with the inhabitants of X—— they shine like diamonds."

" I dare say," I acquiesced. "But I'm not English—I'm American."

"So I perceive from your accent," answered he impertinently. "But as I told you once before, it amounts to the same thing. You wear your rue with a difference, that is all."

"Speaking of sensations," said I, "I would sell my birthright for a cup of coffee."

"You'll find no coffee-house awake at this hour," said Sebastian.

"Then I'll wake one up."

"What! and provoke a violation of the law. By law they're not allowed to open till seven o'clock."

"Oh, laws be hanged! I must have a cup of coffee."

"Really, you are delightful," asserted Sebastian, putting his arm through mine.

Presently we came to a beer hall, at whose door I began to bang. My friend stood by, shaking with laughter, which seemed to me disproportionate to the humour of the event.

"You are easily amused," said I.

"Oh, no, far from it. But this is such a lark you know," said he.

By and by, we were seated opposite each other at a table, sipping hot coffee.

As I looked at Sebastian Roch I observed a startling phenomenon. The apex of his right whisker had become detached from the skin, and was standing out half an inch aloof from his cheek! The sight sent a shiver down my spine. It was certainly most unnatural. His eyes were bright, his voice was soft, he spoke English like a man and a brother, and his character seemed whimsical and open; but his beard, his dashing, black, pointed beard—which I'm not sure I hadn't been envying him a little —was eerie, and, instinctively I felt for my watch. It was safe in its place and so was my purse. Therefore, at the door of the Bierhaus, in due time, we bade each other a friendly good-bye, he promising to look me up one of these days at my hotel.

"I have enjoyed your society more than you can think," he said. "Some of these days I will drop in and see you, *à l'improviste.*"

III

THAT afternoon I again found myself in
the Bischofsplatz, seated at one of the open-
air tables of the café, when a man passed
me, clad in the garb of a Franciscan monk.
He had a pointed black beard, this monk,
and a pair of flashing dark eyes ; and,
though he quickly drew his head into his
cowl at our conjunction, I had no difficulty
whatever in identifying him with my queerly-
hirsute prison mate, Sebastian Roch.

"Dear me ! he has become a monk. It
must have been a swift conversion," thought
I, looking after him.

He marched straight across the Bischofsplatz and into the courtyard of the Marmorhof, where he was lost to view.

"The beggar ! He is one of Conrad's

spies," I concluded; and I searched my memory, to recall if I had said anything that might compromise me in the course of our conversation.

A few hours later I sat down to my dinner in the coffee-room of the Hôtel de Rome, and was about to fall to at the good things before me, when I was arrested in the act by a noise of hurrying feet on the pavement without, and a tumult of excited voices. Something clearly was "up"; and, not to miss it, I hurried to the street-door of the inn.

There I discovered mine host and hostess, supported by the entire *personnel* of their establishment, agape with astonishment, as a loquacious citizen poured news into their ears.

"Otto is dead," said he. "He died at six o'clock. And Conrad has been assassinated. It was between four and five this afternoon. A Franciscan monk presented himself at the Marmorhof, and demanded an

audience of the prince. The guard, of
course, refused him admittance ; but he was
determined, and at last the Prince's Chamberlain gave him a hearing. The upshot
was he wrote a word or two upon a slip of
paper, sealed it with wax, and begged that
it might be delivered to his Highness forth-
with, swearing that it contained information of the utmost importance to his welfare.
The chamberlain conveyed his paper to
the prince, who, directly he had read it,
uttered a great oath, and ordered that the
monk be ushered into his presence, and that
they be left alone together. More than an
hour passed. At a little after six arrived the
news of the death of the old duke. An
officer entered the prince's chamber, to re-
port it to him. There, if you please, he
found his Highness stretched out dead upon
the floor, with a knife in his heart. The
monk had vanished. They could find no
trace whatever of his whereabouts. Also
had vanished the paper he had sent in to

the prince.   But, what the police regard as
an important clue, he had left another paper,
twisted round the handle of the dagger,
whereon was scrawled, in a disguised hand :
' In the country of the blind, it may be, the
one-eyed men are kings, but Conrad only
squinted!'   And now the grand point of it
all is this,—shut up in an inner apartment of
the Marmorhof, they have found the He-
reditary Grand Duchess Mathilde, alive and
well.   Conrad has been keeping her a pris-
oner there these two weeks."

The tidings thus delivered proved to be
correct.   "The Duke is dead! Long live
the Duchess !" cried the populace.

It was like a dear old-fashioned blood-and-
thunder opera, and I was almost behind the
scenes.   But oh, that hypocritical young
fiddler-monk, Sebastian Roch ! Would he
make good his promise, after this, to look
me up ? The police were said to be pro-
secuting a diligent endeavour to look *him*
up, but with, as yet, indifferent success.

Of course, upon the accession of the new
ruler, the print shops of the town displayed
her Highness's portraits for sale—photo-
graphs and chromo-lithographs ; you paid
your money and you took your choice.
These represented her as a slight young
woman, with a delicate, interesting face, a
somewhat sarcastic mouth, a great abun-
dance of yellowish hair, and in striking con-
trast to this, a pair of brilliant dark eyes—
on the whole, a picturesque and pleasing,
if not conventionally a handsome, person.
I could not for the life of me have explained
it, but there was something in her face that
annoyed me with a sense of having seen it
before, though I was sure I never had.   In
the course of a fortnight, however, I did see
her—caught a flying glimpse of her as she
drove through the Marktstrasse in her victoria, attended by all manner of pomp and
circumstance.   She lay back upon her cush-
ions, looking pale and interesting, but sadly
bored, and responded with a languid smile

to the hat-lifting of her subjects. I stared at
her intently, and again I experienced that
exasperating sensation of having seen her
somewhere—where ?—when ?—in what circumstances ?—before.

IV.

ONE night I was awakened from my slumbers by a violent banging at my door.

"Who's there?" I demanded. "What's the matter?"

"Open—open in the name of the law!" commanded a deep bass voice.

"Good heavens! what can the row be now?" I wondered.

"Open, or we break in the door," cried the voice.

"You must really give me time to put something on," I protested, and hurriedly wrapped myself in some clothes.

Then I opened the door.

A magnificently uniformed young officer stepped into the room, followed by three gendarmes with drawn sabres. The officer inclined his head slightly, and said : "Herr Veinricht, ich glaube ? "

His was not the voice that I had heard through the door, gruff and trombone-like, but a much softer voice, and much higher in pitch. Somehow it did not seem altogether the voice of a stranger to me, and yet the face of a stranger his face emphatically was—a very florid face, surmounted by a growth of short red hair, and decorated by a bristling red moustache. His eyes were overhung by bushy red eyebrows, and, in the uncertain candlelight, I could not make out their colour.

"Yes, I am Herr Veinricht," I admitted, resigning myself to this German version of my name.

"English ? " he questioned curtly.

"No, not English—American."

"Macht nichts ! I arrest you in the name of the Grand Duchess."

"Arrest me ! Will you be good enough to inform me upon what charge?"

"Upon the charge of consorting with dangerous characters, and being an enemy to the tranquillity of the State. You will please to dress as quickly as possible. A carriage awaits you below."

"Good Lord! they have somehow connected me with Sebastian Roch," I groaned inwardly. And I began to put certain finishing touches to my toilet.

" No, no," cried the officer. " You must put on your dress-suit. Can you be so ignorant of criminal etiquette as not to know that State prisoners are required to wear their dress-suits ? "

"It seems an absurd regulation," said I, "but I will put on my dress-suit."

" We will await you outside your door ; but let me warn you, should you attempt to escape through your window, you will be shot in a hundred places," said the officer, and retired with his minions.

The whole population of the hotel were in the corridors through which I had pres-

ently to pass with my custodians, and they
pressed after us to the street. A closed carriage stood there, with four horses attached,
each "near" horse bearing a postilion.

Three other horses, saddled, were tied to
posts about the hotel entrance. These the
gendarmes mounted.

"Will you enter the carriage?" said the
officer.

But my spirit rose in arms. "I insist upon knowing what I'm arrested for. I want
to understand the definite nature of the
charge against me."

"I am not a magistrate. Will you kindly enter the carriage?"

"Oh, this is a downright outrage," I declared, and entered the carriage.

The officer leaped in after me, the door was
slammed to, the postilions yelled at their
horses, off we drove, followed by the rhyth-
mical clank-clank of the gendarmes.

"I should like to get at the meaning of all
this, you know," I informed my captor.

"My dear sir, you do not begin to appreciate the premises. One less ignorant of military fashions would have perceived from my coat long since that I am a provost-marshal."

"Well, and what of that? I suppose you are none the less able to explain my position to me."

"Position, sir! This is trifling. But I must caution you that whatever you say will be remembered, and, if incriminating, used against you."

"It is a breach of international comity," said I.

"Oh, we are the best of friends with England," he said, lightly.

"But I am an American, I would have you to know."

"Macht nichts!" said he.

"Macht nichts!" I echoed, angrily. "You think so! I shall bring the case to the notice of the United States Legation, and you shall see."

"How? And precipitate a war between two friendly powers?"

"You laugh! but who laughs last laughs best, and I promise you the Grand Duchy of X—— shall be made to pay for this pleasantry with a vengeance."

"This is not the first time you have been arrested while in these dominions," he said, sternly, "and I must remind you that lèse-majesté is a hanging matter."

"Lèse-majesté!" I repeated, half in scorn, half in terror.

"Ya wohl, mein Herr," he answered. "But, after all, I am simply obeying orders," he added, with an inflection almost apologetic.

Where had I heard of that curious soft voice before? A voice so soft that his German sounded almost like Italian.

Meanwhile we had driven across the town, past the walls, and into the open country.

"You are perhaps conducting me to the

frontier ? " I suggested, deriving some relief from the fancy.

"Oh, hardly so far as that, let us hope," he answered, with what struck me as a suppressed chuckle.

"Far?" I cried. "Can you use the word in speaking of a pocket-handkerchief?"

"It is small, but it is picturesque, it is paintable," said he. "And, what is more, by every syllable you utter against it you weave a strand into your halter, and drive a nail into your coffin. Suicide is imprudent, not to say immoral."

"If I could meet you on equal terms," I cried, "I would pay you for your derision with a good sound Anglo-Saxon thrashing."

"Oh, tiger's heart wrapped in a painter's hide," he retorted, laughing outright.

We drove on in silence for perhaps a quarter of an hour longer ; then at last our horses' hoofs resounded upon stone, and we drew up. My officer descended from the carriage ; I followed him. We were standing under a massive archway lighted by a hanging lantern. Before a small door pierced in the stone wall fronting us a sentinel was posted, with his musket presented in salute.

The three gendarmes sprang from their saddles.

"Farewell, Herr Veinricht," said the provost-marshal. "I have enjoyed our drive together more than I can tell you." Then turning to his subordinates, "Conduct this gentleman to the Tower chamber," he commanded.

One of the gendarmes preceding me, the other two coming behind, I was conveyed up a winding stone staircase, into a big octagonal-shaped room.

The room was lighted by innumerable candles set in sconces round the walls. It was comfortably, even richly furnished, and decorated with a considerable degree of taste. A warm-hued Persian carpet covered the stone floor; books, pictures, bibelots, were scattered discriminatingly about; and in one corner there stood a grand piano, open, with a violin and bow lying on it.

My gendarmes bowed themselves out, shutting the door behind them with an ominous clangour.

"If this is my dungeon cell," I thought, "I shall not be so uncomfortable, after all. But how preposterous of them to force me to wear my dress-suit."

I threw myself into an easy-chair, buried my face in my hands, and tried to reflect upon my situation.

I can't tell how much time may have passed in this way; perhaps twenty minutes or half an hour. Then, suddenly, I was disturbed by the sound of a light little cough behind me, a discreet little "ahem." I looked up quickly. A lady had entered the apartment, and was standing in the middle of it, smiling in contemplation of my desperate attitude.

"Good heavens!" I gasped, but not audibly, as her face grew clear to my startled sight. "The Grand Duchess herself!"

"I am glad to see you, Mr. Wainwright," her Highness began, in English. "X—— is a dull little place—oh, believe me, the dullest of its size in Christendom—and they tell me you are an amusing man. I trust they tell the truth."

Of course the reader has foreseen it from the outset; otherwise why should I be detaining him with this anecdote? But upon me it came as a thunderbolt; and in my emotion I forgot myself, and exclaimed aloud, "Sebastian Roch!" The face of the Grand Duchess had haunted me with a sense of familiarity; the voice of my red-headed officer in the carriage had seemed not strange to me; but now that I saw the face, and heard the voice, at one and the same time, all was clear—"Sebastian Roch!"

"You said——? " the gracious lady questioned, arching her eyes.

" Nothing, madame. I was about to thank your Highness for her kindness, but——"

"But your mind wandered, and you made some irrelevant military observation about a bastion rock. It is, perhaps, aphasia."

"Very probably," I assented.

" But you are a man of honour, are you not? "

" I hope so."

" The English generally are. You can keep a State secret, especially when you happen to have learned it by a sort of accident, can you not? "

" I am a tomb for such things, madame."

"That is well. And besides, you must consider that not all homicide is murder. Sometimes one is driven to kill in self-defence."

" I have not a doubt of that."

"I am only sorry it should all have hap-

pened before you saw him.   His squint
was a rarity ; it would have pleased your
sense of humour.   X—— is the dullest little
principality," she went on, "oh, but dull,
dull, dull !   I am sometimes forced in despair to perpetrate little jokes.   Yet you
have actually stopped here five weeks.   It
must be as they say, that the English people take their pleasures sadly.   You are a
painter, I am told."

"Yes, your Highness ; I make a shift at
painting."

"And I at fiddling.   But I lack a discrim-
inating audience.   I think you had better
paint my portrait.   I will play my fiddle to
you.   Between whiles we will talk.   On occasions, I may tell you, I smoke cigarettes ;
one must have some excitement.   We will
try to enliven things a little.   Do you think
we shall succeed ? "

"Oh, I should not despair of doing so."

"That is nice of you.   I have a most
ridiculous High Chancellor ; you might draw

caricatures of him. And my First Lady of the Chamber has a preposterous lisp. I do hope I shall be amused."

As she spoke, she extended her left hand towards me; I took it, and was about to give it a friendly shake.

"No, no, not that," said she. "Oh, I forgot, you are an American, and the A B C of court etiquette is Sanskrit to you. Must I tell you what to do?"

To cut a long story short, I thought my lines had fallen unto me in extremely pleasant places; and so, indeed, they had—for a while. I passed a merry summer at the Court of X——, alternating between the Residenz in town, and the Schloss beyond the walls. I made a good many preliminary studies for the princess's portrait, whilst she played her violin; and between times, as she had promised, we talked, practised court etiquette, smoked cigarettes, and laughed at scandal. But when I began upon the final canvas, I at least had to become a little

sober.   I wanted to make a masterpiece of
it.   We had two or three sittings, during
which I worked away in grim silence, and
the Grand Duchess yawned.

Then one night I was again roused from
the middle of my slumbers, taken in cus-
tody by a colonel of dragoons, conducted to
a closed carriage, and driven abroad through
the darkness.   When our carriage came to
a standstill we found ourselves in the Aus-
trian village of Z——, beyond the X——
frontier.   There Colonel von Schlangewürtzel
bade me good-bye.   At the same time he
handed me a letter.   I hastened to tear
it open.   Upon a sheet of court paper, in
a pretty feminine hand, I read these words :

"You promised to amuse me.   But it
seems you take your droll British art *au
grand sérieux.*   We have better portrait-
painters among our natives ; and you will
find models cheap and plentiful at Z——.
Farewell !"

𝕿𝖊𝖑𝖊𝖌𝖗𝖆𝖕𝖍𝖎𝖈 𝕬𝖉𝖉𝖗𝖊𝖘𝖘 :
Sunlocks, London.

21 BEDFORD STREET, W.C.
OCTOBER 1892.

A LIST OF

Mr WILLIAM HEINEMANN'S

PUBLICATIONS

AND

FORTHCOMING WORKS

.

𝔍𝔫𝔡𝔢𝔵 of 𝔄𝔲𝔱𝔟𝔬𝔯𝔰.

—•+•—

VICTORIA:
QUEEN AND EMPRESS.
BY
JOHN CORDY JEAFFRESON,
Author of "The Real Lord Byron," etc.

In Two Volumes, 8vo. With Portraits. [*In October.*

TWENTY-FIVE YEARS IN THE SECRET SERVICE.
THE RECOLLECTIONS OF A SPY.
BY
MAJOR LE CARON.
In One Volume, 8vo. With Portraits and Facsimiles.

[*In October.*

REMINISCENCES OF COUNT LEO NICHOLAEVITCH TOLSTOI.
BY
C. A. BEHRS,
TRANSLATED FROM THE RUSSIAN BY
PROFESSOR C. E. TURNER.
In One Volume, Crown 8vo. ⌊*In October.*

THE REALM OF THE HABSBURGS
BY
SIDNEY WHITMAN,
Author of "Imperial Germany."

In One Volume. Crown 8vo. ⌊*In November.*

THE WORKS OF HEINRICH HEINE.   Translated
by CHARLES GODFREY LELAND, M.A., F.R.L.S. (Hans Breitmann).
Crown 8vo, cloth, 5s. per Volume.

I. FLORENTINE NIGHTS, SCHNABELEWOPSKI,
THE RABBI OF BACHARCAH, and SHAKE-
SPEARE'S MAIDENS AND WOMEN.   [*Ready.*

Times.—"We can recommend no better medium for making acquaintance
at first hand with 'the German Aristophanes' than the works of Heinrich
Heine, translated by Charles Godfrey Leland. Mr. Leland manages pretty
successfully to preserve the easy grace of the original."

II., III. PICTURES OF TRAVEL. 1823-1828. In Two
Volumes.   [*Ready.*

Daily Chronicle.—"Mr. Leland's translation of 'The Pictures of Travel'
is one of the acknowledged literary feats of the age. As a traveller Heine is
delicious beyond description, and a volume which includes the magnificent
Lucca series, the North Sea, the memorable Hartz wanderings, must needs
possess an everlasting charm."

IV. THE BOOK OF SONGS.   [*In the Press.*

V., VI. GERMANY. In Two Volumes.   [*Ready.*

Daily Telegraph.—"Mr. Leland has done his translation in able and
scholarly fashion."

VII., VIII. FRENCH AFFAIRS. In Two Volumes.
                                        [*In the Press.*

IX. THE SALON.   [*In preparation.*

₊ *Large Paper Edition, limited to 100 Numbered Copies. Particulars on
application.*

THE POSTHUMOUS WORKS OF THOMAS DE
QUINCEY. Edited with Introduction and Notes from the Author's
Original MSS., by ALEXANDER H. JAPP, LL.D, F.R.S.E., &c. Crown
8vo, cloth, 6s. each.

I. SUSPIRIA DE PROFUNDIS. With Other Essays.

Times.—"Here we have De Quincey at his best. Will be welcome to
lovers of De Quincey and good literature."

II. CONVERSATION AND COLERIDGE. With other
Essays.   [*In preparation.*

The Great Educators.

A Series of Volumes by Eminent Writers, presenting in their entirety "A Biographical History of Education."

The Times.—"A Series of Monographs on 'The Great Educators' should prove of service to all who concern themselves with the history, theory, and practice of education."

The Speaker.—"There is a promising sound about the title of Mr. Heinemann's new series, 'The Great Educators.' It should help to allay the hunger and thirst for knowledge and culture of the vast multitude of young men and maidens which our educational system turns out yearly, provided at least with an appetite for instruction."

Each subject will form a complete volume, crown 8vo, 5*s*.

Now ready.

ARISTOTLE, and the Ancient Educational Ideals. By THOMAS DAVIDSON, M.A., LL.D.

The Times.—"A very readable sketch of a very interesting subject."

LOYOLA, and the Educational System of the Jesuits. By Rev. THOMAS HUGHES, S.J.

Saturday Review.—"Full of valuable information. . . . . If a schoolmaster would learn how the education of the young can be carried on so as to confer real dignity on those engaged in it, we recommend him to read Mr. Hughes' book."

ALCUIN, and the Rise of the Christian Schools. By Professor ANDREW F. WEST, Ph.D.   [*In October.*

In preparation.

ABELARD, and the Origin and Early History of Universities. By JULES GABRIEL COMPAYRÉ, Professor in the Faculty of Toulouse.

ROUSSEAU ; or, Education according to Nature.

HERBART ; or, Modern German Education.

PESTALOZZI ; or, the Friend and Student of Children.

FROEBEL. By H. COURTHOPE BOWEN, M.A.

HORACE MANN, and Public Education in the United States. By NICHOLAS MURRAY BUTLER, Ph.D.

BELL, LANCASTER, and ARNOLD ; or, the English Education of To-Day. By J. G. FITCH, LL.D., Her Majesty's Inspector of Schools.

Others to follow.

THE GREAT WAR OF 189-. A Forecast. By REAR-ADMIRAL COLOMB, COL. MAURICE, R.A., MAJOR HENDERSON, STAFF COLLEGE, CAPTAIN MAUDE, ARCHIBALD FORBES, CHARLES LOWE, D. CHRISTIE MURRAY, F. SCUDAMORE, and SIR CHARLES DILKE. In One Volume, 4to, Illustrated.

In this narrative, which is reprinted from the pages of *Black and White,* an attempt is made to forecast the course of events preliminary and incidental to the Great War which, in the opinion of military and political experts, will probably occur in the immediate future.

The writers, who are well-known authorities on international politics and strategy, have striven to derive the conflict from its most likely source, to conceive the most probable campaigns and acts of policy, and generally to give to their work the verisimilitude and actuality of real warfare. The work has been profusely illustrated from sketches by Mr. Frederic Villiers, the well-known war artist.   *[Nearly ready.*

THE GENTLE ART OF MAKING ENEMIES. As pleasingly exemplified in many instances, wherein the serious ones of this earth, carefully exasperated, have been prettily spurred on to indiscretions and unseemliness, while overcome by an undue sense of right. By J. M'NEIL WHISTLER. *A New Edition.* Pott 4to, half cloth, 10s. 6d.
[Just ready.

Punch.—"The book in itself, in its binding, print and arrangement, is a work of art. . . . . A work of rare humour, a thing of beauty and a joy for now and ever."

THE JEW AT HOME. Impressions of a Summer and Autumn Spent with Him in Austria and Russia. By JOSEPH PENNELL. With Illustrations by the Author. 4to, cloth, 5s.   *[Just ready.*

THE NEW EXODUS. A Study of Israel in Russia. By HAROLD FREDERIC. Demy 8vo, Illustrated. 16s.   *[Just ready.*

PRINCE BISMARCK. An Historical Biography. By CHARLES LOWE, M.A. With Portraits. Crown 8vo, 6s.   *[Just ready.*

The Times.—"Is unquestionably the first important work which deals, fully and with some approach to exhaustiveness, with the career of Bismarck from both the personal and the historical points of view."

ADDRESSES. By HENRY IRVING. Small crown 8vo. With Portrait by J. M'N. Whistler.   *[In the Press.*

STRAY MEMORIES. By ELLEN TERRY. 4to. With Portraits.   *[In preparation.*

LITTLE JOHANNES. By FREDERICK VAN EEDEN. Translated from the Dutch by CLARA BELL. With an Introduction by ANDREW LANG. Illustrated.   *[In preparation.*
  . Also a Large Paper Edition.*

LIFE OF HEINRICH HEINE. By RICHARD GARNETT, LL.D. With Portrait. Crown 8vo (uniform with the translation of Heine's Works).   *[In preparation.*

THE SPEECH OF MONKEYS. By Professor R. L. GARNER. Crown 8vo, 7s. 6d.   *[Just ready.*

Daily Chronicle.—"A real, a remarkable, contribution to our common knowledge."
Daily Telegraph.—"An entertaining book."

THE OLD MAIDS' CLUB. By I. ZANGWILL, Author of "The Bachelors' Club." Illustrated by F. H. TOWNSEND. Crown 8vo, cloth, 3s. 6d.

National Review.—"Mr. Zangwill has a very bright and a very original humour, and every page of this closely printed book is full of point and go, and full, too, of a healthy satire that is really humorously applied common-sense."
Athenæum.—"Most strongly to be recommended to all classes of readers."

WOMAN—THROUGH A MAN'S EYEGLASS. By
MALCOLM C. SALAMAN. With Illustrations by DUDLEY HARDY. Crown 8vo, cloth, 3s. 6d.
Daily Graphic.—" A most amusing book."
Daily Telegraph.—" Written with brightness and elegance, and with touches of bot' caustic satire and kindly humour."
Daily Chronicle.—" It is the very thing for a punt cushion or a garden hammock."

GIRLS AND WOMEN. By E. CHESTER. Pott 8vo, cloth,
2s. 6d., or gilt extra, 3s. 6d.
Literary World.—" We gladly commend this delightful little work to the thoughtful girls of our own country. We hope that many parents and daughters will read and ponder over the little volume."

GOSSIP IN A LIBRARY. By EDMUND GOSSE, Author of
" Northern Studies," &c. Second Edition. Crown 8vo, buckram, gilt top, 7s. 6d.
Athenæum.—" There is a touch of Leigh Hunt in this picture of the book-lover among his books, and the volume is one that Leigh Hunt would have delighted in."
. Large Paper Edition, limited to 100 Numbered Copies, 25s. net.

THE LIFE OF HENRIK IBSEN. By HENRIK JÆGER.
Translated by CLARA BELL. With the Verse done into English from the Norwegian Original by EDMUND GOSSE. Crown 8vo, cloth, 6s.
Academy.—" We welcome it heartily. An unqualified boon to the many English students of Ibsen."

DE QUINCEY MEMORIALS. Being Letters and other
Records here first Published, with Communications from COLERIDGE, The WORDSWORTHS, HANNAH MORE, PROFESSOR WILSON and others. Edited, with Introduction, Notes, and Narrative, by ALEXANDER H. JAPP, LL.D. F.R.S.E. In two volumes, demy 8vo, cloth, with portraits, 30s. net.
Daily Telegraph.—" Few works of greater literary interest have of late years issued from the press than the two volumes of ' De Quincey Memorials.' They comprise most valuable materials for the historian of literary and social England at the beginning of the century; but they are not on that account less calculated to amuse, enlighten, and absorb the general reader of biographical memoirs."

THE WORD OF THE LORD UPON THE WATERS.
Sermons read by His Imperial Majesty the Emperor of Germany, while at Sea on his Voyages to the Land of the Midnight Sun. Composed by Dr. RICHTER, Army Chaplain, and Translated from the German by JOHN R. MCILRAITH. 4to, cloth, 2s. 6d.
Times.—" The Sermons are vigorous, simple, and vivid in themselves, and well adapted to the circumstances in which they were delivered."

THE HOURS OF RAPHAEL, IN OUTLINE.
Together with the Ceiling of the Hall where they were originally painted. By MARY E. WILLIAMS. Folio, cloth, £2 2s. net.

THE PASSION PLAY AT OBERAMMERGAU, 1890.
By F. W. FARRAR, D.D., F.R.S., Archdeacon and Canon of Westminster &c. &c. 4to, cloth, 2s. 6d.
Spectator.—" This little book will be read with delight by those who have, and by those who have not, visited Oberammergau."

THE GARDEN'S STORY; or, Pleasures and Trials of an
Amateur Gardener. By G. H. ELLWANGER. With an Introduction by the Rev. C. WOLLEY DOD. 12mo, cloth, with Illustrations, 5s.
Scotsman.—" It deals with a charming subject in a charming manner."

IDLE MUSINGS: Essays in Social Mosaic. By E. CONDER
GRAY, Author of " Wise Words and Loving Deeds," &c. &c. Crown 8vo, cloth. 6s.
Saturday Review.—" Light, brief, and bright."

THE COMING TERROR. And other Essays and Letters.

By ROBERT BUCHANAN. Second Edition. Demy 8vo, cloth, 12s. 6d.

Daily Chronicle.—"This amusing, wrong-headed, audacious, 'cranky' book should be widely read, for there is not a dull line in it."

ARABIC AUTHORS: A Manual of Arabian History and

Literature. By F. F. ARBUTHNOT, M.R.A.S., Author of "Early Ideas," "Persian Portraits," &c. 8vo, cloth, 10s.

Manchester Examiner.—"The whole work has been carefully indexed, and will prove a handbook of the highest value to the student who wishes to gain a better acquaintance with Arabian letters "

THE LABOUR MOVEMENT IN AMERICA. By

RICHARD T. ELY, Ph.D., Associate in Political Economy, Johns Hopkins University. Crown 8vo, cloth, 5s.

Saturday Review.—"Both interesting and valuable.

THE LITTLE MANX NATION. (Lectures delivered at

the Royal Institution, 1891.) By HALL CAINE, Author of "The Bond-man," "The Scapegoat," &c. Crown 8vo, cloth, 3s. 6d.; paper, 2s. 6d.

World.—"Mr. Hall Caine takes us back to the days of old romance, and, treating tradition and history in the pictorial style of which he is a master, he gives us a monograph of Man especially acceptable."

NOTES FOR THE NILE. Together with a Metrical

Rendering of the Hymns of Ancient Egypt and of the Precepts of Ptah-hotep (the oldest book in the world). By HARDWICKE D. RAWNSLEY, M.A. 16mo, cloth, 5s.

The Times.—"All visitors to Egypt will find much instruction and enter-tainment pleasantly conveyed."

Saturday Review.—"A pleasant and useful little companion for the culti-vated traveller."

DENMARK: Its History, Topography, Language, Literature,

Fine Arts, Social Life, and Finance. Edited by H. WEITEMEYER. Demy 8vo, cloth, with Map, 12s. 6d.

*** *Dedicated, by permission, to H.R.H. the Princess of Wales.*

Morning Post.—"An excellent account of everything relating to this Northern country."

IMPERIAL GERMANY. A Critical Study of Fact and

Character. By SIDNEY WHITMAN. New Edition, Revised and Enlarged. Crown 8vo, cloth 2s. 6d.; paper, 2s.

Prince Bismarck.—"I consider the different chapters of this book masterly."

THE CANADIAN GUIDE-BOOK. Part I. The Tourist's

and Sportsman's Guide to Eastern Canada and Newfoundland, including full descriptions of Routes, Cities, Points of Interest, Summer Resorts, Fishing Places, &c., in Eastern Ontario, The Muskoka District, The St. Lawrence Region, The Lake St. John Country, The Maritime Provinces, Prince Edward Island, and Newfoundland. With an Appendix giving Fish and Game Laws, and Official Lists of Trout and Salmon Rivers and their Lessees. By CHARLES G. D. ROBERTS, Professor of English Literature in King's College, Windsor, N.S. With Maps and many Illustrations. Crown 8vo, limp cloth, 6s.

Part II. WESTERN CANADA. Including the Peninsula

and Northern Regions of Ontario, the Canadian Shores of the Great Lakes, the Lake of the Woods Region, Manitoba and "The Great North-West," The Canadian Rocky Mountains and National Park, British Columbia, and Vancouver Island. By ERNEST INGERSOLL. With Maps and many Illustrations. Crown 8vo, limp cloth. [*In preparation.*

𝔉iction.

In Three Volumes.

THE HEAD OF THE FIRM. By Mrs. RIDDELL, Author
of " George Geith," " Maxwell Drewett," &c. [*Just ready.*

CHILDREN OF THE GHETTO. By I. ZANGWILL,
Author of " The Old Maids' Club," &c. [*Just ready.*

THE TOWER OF TADDEO. A Novel. By OUIDA,
Author of "Two Little Wooden Shoes," &c. [*In October.*

KITTY'S FATHER. By FRANK BARRETT. Author of
" Lieutenant Barnabas," &c. [*In November.*

THE COUNTESS RADNA. By W. E. NORRIS, Author of
" Matrimony," &c. [*In January.*

ORIOLE'S DAUGHTER. A Novel. By JESSIE FOTHERGILL,
Author of " The First Violin," &c. [*In February.*

THE LAST SENTENCE. By MAXWELL GRAY, Author of
" The Silence of Dean Maitland," &c. [*In March.*

In Two Volumes.

WOMAN AND THE MAN. A Love Story. By ROBERT
BUCHANAN, Author of " Come Live with Me and be My Love," " The
Moment After," " The Coming Terror," &c. [*In preparation.*

A KNIGHT OF THE WHITE FEATHER. By " TASMA,"
Author of "The Penance of Portia James," "Uncle Piper of Piper's
Hill," &c. [*Just ready.*

A LITTLE MINX. By ADA CAMBRIDGE, Author of "A
Marked Man," "The Three Miss Kings," &c.

In One Volume.

THE NAULAHKA. A Tale of West and East. By RUDYARD
KIPLING and WOLCOTT BALESTIER. Crown 8vo, cloth, 6s. Second
Edition. [*Just ready.*

THE AVERAGE WOMAN. By WOLCOTT BALESTIER.
With an Introduction by HENRY JAMES. Small crown 8vo, 3s. 6d.
[*Just ready.*

THE ATTACK ON THE MILL and Other Sketches
of War. By EMILE ZOLA. With an essay on the short stories of M.
Zola by Edmund Gosse. Small crown 8vo, 3s. 6d. [*Just ready.*

DUST. By BJÖRNSTJERNE BJÖRNSON. Translated from the
Norwegian. Small crown 8vo.

THE SECRET OF NARCISSE. By EDMUND GOSSE.
Crown 8vo. [*In October.*

MADEMOISELLE MISS and Other Stories. By HENRY
HARLAND, Author of " Mea Culpa," &c. Small crown 8vo. [*In the Press.*

THE DOMINANT SEVENTH. A Musical Story. By
KATE ELIZABETH CLARKE. Crown 8vo, cloth, 5s.
Speaker.—" A very romantic story."

PASSION THE PLAYTHING. A Novel. By R. MURRAY
GILCHRIST. Crown 8vo, cloth, 6s.
Athenæum.—" This well-written story must be read to be appreciated."

The Crown Copyright Series.

Mr. HEINEMANN has made arrangements with a number of the FIRST AND MOST POPULAR ENGLISH, AMERICAN, and COLONIAL AUTHORS which will enable him to issue a series of NEW AND ORIGINAL WORKS, to be known as THE CROWN COPYRIGHT SERIES, complete in One Volume, at a uniform price of FIVE SHILLINGS EACH. These Novels will not pass through an Expensive Two or Three Volume Edition, but they will be obtainable at the CIRCULATING LIBRARIES, as well as at all Booksellers' and Bookstalls.

ACCORDING TO ST. JOHN. By AMÉLIE RIVES, Author
of "The Quick or the Dead."

Scotsman.—"The literary work is highly artistic. . . . . It has beauty and brightness, and a kind of fascination which carries the reader on till he has read to the last page."

THE PENANCE OF PORTIA JAMES. By TASMA,
Author of "Uncle Piper of Piper's Hill," &c.

Athenæum.—"A powerful novel."
Daily Chronicle.—"Captivating and yet tantalising, this story is far above the average."
Vanity Fair.—"A very interesting story, morally sound, and flavoured throughout with ease of diction and lack of strain."

INCONSEQUENT LIVES. A Village Chronicle, shewing
how certain folk set out for El Dorado; what they attempted; and what they attained. By J. H. PEARCE, Author of "Esther Pentreath," &c.

Saturday Review.—"A vivid picture of the life of Cornish fisher-folk. It is unquestionably interesting."

Literary World.—"Powerful and pathetic . . . . from first to last it is profoundly interesting. It is long since we read a story revealing power of so high an order, marked by such evident carefulness of workmanship, such skill in the powerful and yet temperate presentation of passion, and in the sternly realistic yet delicate treatment of difficult situations."

A QUESTION OF TASTE. By MAARTEN MAARTENS,
Author of "An Old Maid's Love," &c.

National Observer.—"There is more than cleverness; there is original talent, and a good deal of humanity besides."

COME LIVE WITH ME AND BE MY LOVE. By
ROBERT BUCHANAN, Author of "The Moment After," "The Coming Terror," &c.

Globe.—"Will be found eminently readable."
Daily Telegraph.—"We will conclude this brief notice by expressing our cordial admiration of the skill displayed in its construction, and the genial humanity that has inspired its author in the shaping and vitalising of the individuals created by his fertile imagination."

THE O'CONNORS OF BALLINAHINCH. By Mrs.
HUNGERFORD, Author of "Molly Bawn," &c.   [*In the Press.*

A BATTLE AND A BOY. By BLANCHE WILLIS HOWARD,
Author of "Guenn," &c.   [*In preparation.*

VANITAS. By VERNON LEE, Author of "Hauntings," &c.
[*In preparation.*

Ibeinemann's International Xibrarp.

EDITED BY EDMUND GOSSE.

New Review.—" If you have any pernicious remnants of literary chauvinism I hope it will not survive the series of foreign classics of which Mr. William Heinemann, aided by Mr. Edmund Gosse, is publishing translations to the great contentment of all lovers of literature."

Times.—" A venture which deserves encouragement."

Each Volume has an Introduction specially written by the Editor.

Price, in paper covers, 2s. 6d. each, or cloth, 3s. 6d.

IN GOD'S WAY. From the Norwegian of BJÖRNSTJERNE BJÖRNSON.

Athenæum.—" Without doubt the most important and the most interesting work published during the twelve months. . . . . There are descriptions which certainly belong to the best and cleverest things our literature has ever produced. Amongst the many characters, the doctor's wife is unquestionably the first. It would be difficult to find anything more tender, soft, and refined than this charming personage."

PIERRE AND JEAN. From the French of GUY DE MAU-PASSANT.

Pall Mall Gazette.—" So fine and faultless, so perfectly balanced, so steadily progressive, so clear and simple and satisfying. It is admirable from beginning to end."

Athenæum.—" Ranks amongst the best gems of modern French fiction."

THE CHIEF JUSTICE. From the German of KARL EMIL FRANZOS, Author of " For the Right," &c.

New Review.—" Few novels of recent times have a more sustained and vivid human interest."

Christian World.—" A story of wonderful power . . . . as free from any-thing objectionable as ' The Heart of Midlothian.' "

WORK WHILE YE HAVE THE LIGHT. From the Russian of Count LYOF TOLSTOY.

Liverpool Mercury.—" Marked by all the old power of the great Russian novelist."

Manchester Guardian.—" Readable and well translated ; full of high and noble feeling."

FANTASY. From the Italian of MATILDE SERAO.

National Observer.—" The strongest work from the hand of a woman that has been published for many a day."

Scottish Leader.—" The book is full of a glowing and living realism. . . . . There is nothing like ' Fantasy ' in modern literature. . . . . It is a work of elfish art, a mosaic of light and love, of right and wrong, of human weakness and strength, and purity and wantonness, pieced together in deft and witching precision."

FROTH. From the Spanish of Don ARMANDO PALACIO-VALDÉS.

Daily Telegraph.—" Vigorous and powerful in the highest degree. It abounds in forcible delineation of character, and describes scenes with rare and graphic strength."

FOOTSTEPS OF FATE. From the Dutch of LOUIS COUPERUS.

Daily Chronicle.—" A powerfully realistic story which has been excellently translated."

Gentlewoman.—" The consummate art of the writer prevents this tragedy from sinking to melodrama. Not a single situation is forced or a circumstance exaggerated."

Ibeinemann's 3nternational %ibrary.

PEPITA JIMÉNEZ. From the Spanish of JUAN VALERA.

New Review (Mr. George Saintsbury):—"There is no doubt at all that it is one of the best stories that have appeared in any country in Europe for the last twenty years."

THE COMMODORE'S DAUGHTERS. From the Norwegian of JONAS LIE.

Athenæum.—"Everything that Jonas Lie writes is attractive and pleasant; the plot of deeply human interest, and the art noble."

THE HERITAGE OF THE KURTS. From the Norwegiar of BJÖRNSTJERNE BJÖRNSON.

Pall Mall Gazette.—"A most fascinating as well as a powerful book."
National Observer.—"It is a book to read and a book to think about, for, incontestably, it is the work of a man of genius."

In the Press.

LOU. From the German of BARON V. ROBERTS.

DONA LUZ. From the Spanish of JUAN VALERA.

WITHOUT DOGMA. From the Polish of H. SIENKIEWICZ.

popular 3s. 60. ftovels.

CAPT'N DAVY'S HONEYMOON, The Blind Mother, and The Last Confession. By HALL CAINE, Author of "The Bondman," "The Scapegoat," &c.

THE SCAPEGOAT. By HALL CAINE, Author of "The Bondman," &c.

Mr. Gladstone writes:—"I congratulate you upon 'The Scapegoat' as a work of art, and especially upon the noble and skilfully drawn character of Israel."
Times.—"In our judgment it excels in dramatic force all his previous efforts. For grace and touching pathos Naomi is a character which any romancist in the world might be proud to have created."

THE BONDMAN. A New Saga. By HALL CAINE. Twentieth Thousand.

Mr. Gladstone.—"'The Bondman' is a work of which I recognise the freshness, vigour, and sustained interest no less than its integrity of aim."
Standard.—"Its argument is grand, and it is sustained with a power that is almost marvellous."

DESPERATE REMEDIES. By THOMAS HARDY, Author of "Tess of the D'Urbervilles," &c.

Saturday Review.—"A remarkable story worked out with abundant skill."

A MARKED MAN: Some Episodes in his Life. By ADA CAMBRIDGE, Author of "Two Years' Time," "A Mere Chance," &c.

Morning Post.—"A depth of feeling, a knowledge of the human heart, and an amount of tact that one rarely finds. Should take a prominent place among the novels of the season."

THE THREE MISS KINGS. By ADA CAMBRIDGE, Author of "A Marked Man."

Athenæum.—"A charming study of character. The love stories are excellent, and the author is happy in tender situations."

NOT ALL IN VAIN. By ADA CAMBRIDGE, Author of "A Marked Man," "The Three Miss Kings," &c.

Guardian.—"A clever and absorbing story."
Queen.—"All that remains to be said is 'read the book.'"

Popular 3s. 6d. Novels.

UNCLE PIPER OF PIPER'S HILL. By TASMA. New Popular Edition.

Guardian.—" Every page of it contains good wholesome food, which demands and repays digestion. The tale itself is thoroughly charming, and all the characters are delightfully drawn. We strongly recommend all lovers of wholesome novels to make acquaintance with it themselves, and are much mistaken if they do not heartily thank us for the introduction."

IN THE VALLEY. By HAROLD FREDERIC, Author of "The Lawton Girl," "Seth's Brother's Wife," &c. With Illustrations.

Times.—" The literary value of the book is high ; the author's studies of bygone life presenting a life-like picture."

PRETTY MISS SMITH. By FLORENCE WARDEN, Author of "The House on the Marsh," "A Witch of the Hills," &c.

Punch.—" Since Miss Florence Warden's ' House on the Marsh,' I have not read a more exciting tale."

NOR WIFE, NOR MAID. By Mrs. HUNGERFORD, Author of " Molly Bawn," &c.

Queen.—" It has all the characteristics of the writer's work, and greater emotional depth than most of its predecessors."
Scotsman.—" Delightful reading, supremely interesting."

MAMMON. A Novel. By Mrs. ALEXANDER, Author of "The Wooing O't," &c.

Scotsman.—" The present work is not behind any of its predecessors. 'Mammon ' is a healthy story, and as it has been thoughtfully written it has the merit of creating thought in its readers."

DAUGHTERS OF MEN. By HANNAH LYNCH, Author of " The Prince of the Glades," &c.

Daily Telegraph.—" Singularly clever and fascinating."
Academy.—" One of the cleverest, if not also the pleasantest, stories that have appeared for a long time."

A ROMANCE OF THE CAPE FRONTIER. By BERTRAM MITFORD, Author of "Through the Zulu Country," &c.

Observer.—" This is a rattling tale, genial, healthy, and spirited."

'TWEEN SNOW AND FIRE. A Tale of the Kafir War of 1877. By BERTRAM MITFORD.

THE MASTER OF THE MAGICIANS. By ELIZABETH STUART PHELPS and HERBERT D. WARD.

Athenæum.—" A thrilling story."

LOS CERRITOS. A Romance of the Modern Time. By GERTRUDE FRANKLIN ATHERTON, Author of "Hermia Suydam," and " What Dreams may Come."

Athenæum.—" Full of fresh fancies and suggestions. Told with strength and delicacy. A decidedly charming romance."

A MODERN MARRIAGE. By the Marquise CLARA LANZA

Queen.—" A powerful story, dramatically and consistently carried out."
Black and White.—" A decidedly clever book."

Popular Shilling Books.

MADAME VALERIE. By F. C. PHILIPS, Author of "As in a Looking-Glass," &c.

THE MOMENT AFTER: A Tale of the Unseen. By ROBERT BUCHANAN.

Athenæum.—"Should be read—in daylight."
Observer.—"A clever *tour de force.*"
Guardian.—"Particularly impressive, graphic, and powerful."

CLUES; or, Leaves from a Chief Constable's Note-Book. By WILLIAM HENDERSON, Chief Constable of Edinburgh.

Mr. Gladstone.—"I found the book full of interest."

A VERY STRANGE FAMILY. By F. W. ROBINSON, Author of "Grandmother's Money," "Lazarus in London," &c.

Glasgow Herald.—"An ingeniously devised plot, of which the interest is kept up to the very last page. A judicious blending of humour and pathos further helps to make the book delightful reading from start to finish."

Dramatic Literature.

THE PLAYS OF ARTHUR W. PINERO.

With Introductory Notes by MALCOLM C. SALAMAN. 16mo, Paper Covers, 1s. 6d.; or Cloth, 2s. 6d. each.

THE TIMES: A Comedy in Four Acts. With a Preface by the Author. (Vol. I.)

Daily Telegraph.—"'The Times' is the best example yet given of Mr. Pinero's power as a satirist. So clever is his work that it beats down opposition. So fascinating is his style that we cannot help listening to him."

Morning Post.—"Mr. Pinero's latest belongs to a high order of dramatic literature, and the piece will be witnessed again with all the greater zest after the perusal of such admirable dialogue."

THE PROFLIGATE: A Play in Four Acts. With Portrait of the Author, after J. MORDECAI. (Vol. II.)

Pall Mall Gazette.—"Will be welcomed by all who have the true interests of the stage at heart."

THE CABINET MINISTER: A Farce in Four Acts. (Vol. III.)

Observer.—"It is as amusing to read as it was when played."

THE HOBBY HORSE: A Comedy in Three Acts. (Vol. IV.)

St. James's Gazette.—"Mr. Pinero has seldom produced better or more interesting work than in 'The Hobby Horse.'"

LADY BOUNTIFUL. A Play in Four Acts. (Vol. V.)

THE MAGISTRATE. A Farce in Three Acts. (Vol. VI.)

To be followed by Dandy Dick, The Schoolmistress, The Weaker Sex, Lords and Commons, The Squire, and Sweet Lavender.

Dramatic Literature.

A NEW PLAY. By HENRIK IBSEN. Translated from the Norwegian. Small 4to. *[In preparation.*

A NEW PLAY. By BJÖRNSTJERNE BJÖRNSON. Translated from the Norwegian. *[In preparation.*

THE PRINCESSE MALEINE: A Drama in Five Acts (Translated by Gerard Harry), and THE INTRUDER: A Drama in One Act. By MAURICE MAETERLINCK. With an Introduction by HALL CAINE, and a Portrait of the Author. Small 4to, cloth, 5s.

, *Athenæum.*—"In the creation of the 'atmosphere' of the play M. Maeterlinck shows his skill. It is here that he communicates to us the *nouveau frisson,* here that he does what no one else has done. In 'The Intruder' the art consists of the subtle gradations of terror, the slow, creeping progress of the nightmare of apprehension. Nothing quite like it has been done before—not even by Poe—not even by Villiers."

THE FRUITS OF ENLIGHTENMENT: A Comedy in Four Acts. By Count LYOF TOLSTOY. Translated from the Russian by E. J. DILLON. With Introduction by A. W. PINERO. Small 4to, with Portrait, 5s.

Pall Mall Gazette.—"The whole effect of the play is distinctly Molièresque; it has something of the large humanity of the master. Its satire is genial, almost gay."

HEDDA GABLER: A Drama in Four Acts. By HENRIK IBSEN. Translated from the Norwegian by EDMUND GOSSE. Small 4to, cloth, with Portrait, 5s. Vaudeville Edition, paper, 1s. Also a Limited Large Paper Edition, 21s. *net.*

Times.—"The language in which this play is couched is a model of brevity, decision, and pointedness. . . . . Every line tells, and there is not an incident that does not bear on the action immediate or remote. As a corrective to the vapid and foolish writing with which the stage is deluged 'Hedda Gabler' is perhaps entitled to the place of honour."

STRAY MEMORIES. By ELLEN TERRY. In one volume. Illustrated. *[In preparation.*

SOME INTERESTING FALLACIES OF THE Modern Stage. An Address delivered to the Playgoers' Club at St. James's Hall, on Sunday, 6th December, 1891. By HERBERT BEERBOHM TREE. Crown 8vo, sewed, 6d.

THE LIFE OF HENRIK IBSEN. By HENRIK JÆGER. Translated by CLARA BELL. With the Verse done into English from the Norwegian Original by EDMUND GOSSE. Crown 8vo, cloth, 6s.

St. James's Gazette.—"Admirably translated. Deserves a cordial and emphatic welcome."

Guardian.—"Ibsen's dramas at present enjoy a considerable vogue, and their admirers will rejoice to find full descriptions and criticisms in Mr. Jæger's book."

Poetry.

IVY AND PASSION FLOWER: Poems.   By GERARD
BENDALL, Author of " Estelle," &c. &c.   12mo, cloth, 3s. 6d.

Scotsman.—" Will be read with pleasure."
Musical World.—" The poems are delicate specimens of art, graceful and polished."

VERSES.   By GERTRUDE HALL.   12mo, cloth, 3s. 6d.

Manchester Guardian.—" Will be welcome to every lover of poetry who takes it up.'

MAGONIA: A Poem.   By CHARLES GODFREY LELAND (HANS
BREITMANN).   Fcap. 8vo.   [*In the Press.*

IDYLLS OF WOMANHOOD.   By C. AMY DAWSON.
Fcap. 8vo, gilt top, 5s.

Heinemann's Scientific Handbooks.

MANUAL OF BACTERIOLOGY.   By A. B. GRIFFITHS,
Ph.D., F.R.S. (Edin.), F.C.S.   Crown 8vo, cloth, Illustrated.
                                                           [*In the Press.*
MANUAL OF ASSAYING GOLD, SILVER, COPPER,
and Lead Ores.   By WALTER LEE BROWN, B.Sc.   Revised, Corrected,
and considerably Enlarged, with a chapter on the Assaying of Fuel, &c.
By A. B. GRIFFITHS, Ph.D., F.R.S. (Edin.), F.C.S.   Crown 8vo, cloth,
Illustrated, 7s. 6d.

Colliery Guardian.—" A delightful and fascinating book."
Financial World.—" The most complete and practical manual on everything which concerns assaying of all which have come before us."

GEODESY.   By J. HOWARD GORE.   Crown 8vo, cloth, Illustrated, 5s.

St. James's Gazette.—" The book may be safely recommended to those who desire to acquire an accurate knowledge of Geodesy."
Science Gossip.—" It is the best we could recommend to all geodetic students. It is full and clear, thoroughly accurate, and up to date in all matters of earth-measurements."

THE PHYSICAL PROPERTIES OF GASES.   By
ARTHUR L. KIMBALL, of the Johns Hopkins University.   Crown 8vo,
cloth, Illustrated, 5s.

Chemical News.—" The man of culture who wishes for a general and accurate acquaintance with the physical properties of gases, will find in Mr. Kimball's work just what he requires."

HEAT AS A FORM OF ENERGY.   By Professor R. H.
THURSTON, of Cornell University.   Crown 8vo, cloth, Illustrated, 5s.

Manchester Examiner.—" Bears out the character of its predecessors for careful and correct statement and deduction under the light of the most recent discoveries."

LONDON:

WILLIAM HEINEMANN,

21 BEDFORD STREET, W.C.

www.ingramcontent.com/pod-product-compliance
Lightning Source LLC
Chambersburg PA
CBHW020615030726
47497CB00007B/2251